RUTHLESS HEART

RUTHLESS: BOOK 1

ROXY SLOANE

ROXY SLOANE BOOKS

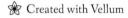

ALSO BY ROXY SLOANE

Ruthless: Book One

Ruthless Heart

He was the boy I loved. Now, he's the man who wants me dead.

Nero Barretti is a Mafia prince. Ruthless. Revered.

And the man who controls my fate.

For ten years, I've been running from our past, but now there's no escape.

To save my family, I'll have to risk it all.

An impossible bargain.

An unstoppable passion.

But there's a thin line between hate... And **desire**.

THE FLAWLESS SERIES:

NERO

FORGET ABOUT FLOWERS AND CANDY. Romance is for men who don't know how to fuck.

You know what I'm talking about: Face down on the mattress, ass up, just begging for a smack. A heavy weight pinning you down, a rough hand knotted in your hair. That thick, straining cock pounding into you, relentless. Almost too much, too big, to take.

But you take it, don't you? Like you were made for every inch. Writhing. Clawing the sheets. Screaming the whole fucking neighborhood down, because you've never had it this good before.

You've never had a man like *me*.

Because I know what you've been dreaming about. A man who takes what he wants. No apologies, no remorse. A man who lives in the shadows, who'll give it to you dirty, like the animal you really are.

Beneath the pretty manners, and charming smiles, you want to be ravaged. Rode hard. *Possessed.*

Like her.

She was my first love, and my wildest obsession. Her innocence drove me to the brink of madness, and even now, I still hear her in the night: Moaning my name as her body surrendered and her sweet pussy seized around my cock.

The taste of her was intoxicating. Her betrayal lives on like a poison in my veins.

For ten long years I've searched for her, waiting for the day when I can have my revenge. Break her the same way she left me broken. Drive her to insanity with desire, the way she did to me.

An eye for an eye. A heart for a heart.

She will be mine.

1

LILY

IT'S two a.m. on a Wednesday morning when a man walks through the door and ruins my life.

You might think there isn't much in my life left to ruin, since I'm serving drunk assholes watered down whiskey in a strip club on the outskirts of Las Vegas, and maybe you're right. I'm not curing cancer, or fighting for world peace, and the only masterpiece I'm painting is the lipsticked smile on my face, inviting guys to shove grubby singles in the waistband of my leather miniskirt. The nuns at my old fancy Catholic school would probably faint if they could see me now—and then pray for my poor soul.

No, this life isn't anything like the one I dreamed about, but it's just that: a life. And it's a hell of a lot better than the alternative, which is laying six feet under in an unmarked grave somewhere like I never even existed at all.

The Barretti Family doesn't give you the honor of a headstone, not when you've crossed them like I have.

Which is why I take one look at the guy who just sauntered in, and my blood runs cold.

You knew this day would come.

I look again, praying that I've got it wrong, that I'm just seeing things in the dim light, but I would know that man blindfolded at a hundred paces.

Nero Barretti.

I panic.

He hasn't seen me, he's too busy frowning at his cellphone, surrounded by a group of his guys. I even recognize a few of them, checking out the dancers on stage, shaking their asses to Rihanna. The group flags down a waitress, joking about something; the fat wad of bills in their hands say that they're here to play. But there's only one man who matters to me. Nero. He's still looking at his phone, distracted.

And then, I realize: They haven't come here looking for me.

I still have a chance.

I duck through the crowd, drunk and rowdy like usual. I keep my head down, away from the threat, cursing my bad luck.

Of all the shitty strip clubs in Vegas, he had to walk into mine.

"Amber!" One of the other girls catches me by the bar. "Where are you going? You're supposed to close at four."

Fuck.

"Cover me?" I ask, pleading. I shoot an anxious look back across the room, but I don't see him. "I'm... Not feeling great."

She sighs. "I don't know..."

"You can take my tips for the night," I say, pulling loose bills from the stash in my bra. "I'll close the rest of the week. Whatever you want."

"Fine," she agrees, then studies me. "You should get home. You don't look so hot."

I don't feel it either. "I owe you!" I tell her, grateful, and hurry towards the back exit, already knowing I won't be back.

Amber will fade away as easily as I invented her. Just another fake name to add to the list of women that I used to be.

I head down a dark hallway, and out the back door into the alley. I can see the neon lights flickering from the Strip and take a deep breath of relief. *Freedom.* But I've only made it a few steps, when someone grabs me from behind.

I freeze in fear, turning—but it's one of the customers from inside.

"Baby, where you goin'?" he slurs, eyes unfocused. But his hand is focused all right—right on my ass.

"Sorry!" I blurt, trying to slip under his grabby hands, but the guy holds on tight. He backs me up against the wall, beside the trash cans.

"How much for a dance?" he leers down at me, breath rancid.

I try not to retch. "I'm not a dancer, I just serve the drinks," I say, putting my hands on his chest and trying to push him away. But the guy's built like a linebacker.

"So maybe we don't dance..." Bad Breath shoves me back against the wall. My shoulder hits the brick painfully, and I yelp, but he doesn't seem to notice. Or care.

He leans in to nuzzle at my hair, pressing closer, pinning me in place so I can't move. His hand gropes my breast, and I struggle in revulsion, looking over his shoulder to see if Security is around to toss this guy like usual.

But it's not a friendly face that steps out the back door.

It's him.

Nero's making a call on his cell phone, his voice steady and lethal. The light catches his face properly for the first time, and I stifle a gasp. In the ten years since I saw him last, I've thought of him a million times. But I've been picturing the boy he used to be at twenty. Lanky, still filling out; a mop of dark curls, and a boyish smile that could tempt you into breaking all the rules.

But the man staring in the doorway is cut from raw steel. Hard and unflinching. He looms there, muscles taut against the fabric of his black T-shirt and jeans; mottled tattoos spilling up his neck. He's unshaven, his hair tousled, and his eyes full of contempt as he barks an order on the phone.

I feel an ache, memories rushing back like a tidal wave. But I force them back. I can't go down that road, not right now, shoved up against the wall with this drunk asshole about to give the game away.

About to end my shitty life forever.

"Yeah, baby..." The drunk guy's hand moves between us, and I hear the sound of his zipper. I fight the rising bile in my throat. Nero is still standing there oblivious, barely twenty feet away from us.

He hasn't noticed us here in the shadow of the dumpster, but if I struggle... If I scream...

He'll hear me.

And then it'll all be over.

In a split-second, I weigh the impossible choice. Either I let this drunk guy rape me here in the alleyway...

Or Nero Barretti will find out exactly where I disappeared to. And not just me, either.

He'll find my little brother, too.

God help me.

I close my eyes, tears hot on my cheeks as I sink back against the wall.

Make it fast, I pray. *Just get it over with.*

The drunk guy is pawing at me, breathing faster now in anticipation. "Baby, yeah..." he groans, yanking my skirt higher. "I know you want it."

What I want is the past ten years of my life back. To be somewhere far away from this grimy alley, and these grubby hands, making impossible choices just to stay alive.

"Fuck," he groans, fumbling with his limp whiskey dick. "Just gimme a sec, I'm getting harder, I'm getting—"

Just like that, he's gone.

My eyes fly open in time to see Nero hurl the guy to the ground and bring his heel down on the man's head with a sickening crunch.

"Hands off the merchandise." Nero tells him coldly. "This one's taken."

He gives me an assessing look, like there's not a decade of history between us. "Lily Fordham," he says coolly, eyes lingering on my ripped blouse and hiked-up skirt. "I never thought I'd see the day."

I'm reeling from the icy scorn in his gaze, but Drunk Guy isn't out yet. He lurches to his feet, roaring angrily, and lunges at Nero. Caught off guard, Nero stumbles back, and the guys go careening into the dumpsters.

I don't wait around for another second. I take off, my heels clattering on the asphalt as I bomb it across the parking lot to my ancient Jetta. I pull my keys from the pouch around my waist and jam them into the ignition, hands shaking so hard it takes me three tries just to get them in.

The engine sputters.

"Please start, please start."

I chant it, sobbing, until finally it bursts to life. I pull away, tires screeching, damn near breaking the speed limit driving across town until I pull up outside my rundown apartment complex and race inside. I hurry up the stairs to my floor, and slam the door behind me, shoving the deadbolt into place.

I sink to the floor, my heart pounding.

What do I do now?

I look around. The place is sparsely furnished, but I've done my best to make it feel like home:thrifted furniture, books, and blankets. I painted the kitchen sunbeam yellow and did a mural on the bedroom walls: Jungle vines twisting up to a blue ceiling, tropical and bright.

But a part of me always knew it would be temporary.

A part of me always knew, the day would come when I would have to leave it all behind.

Once it would have been for him. *With him.*

Now, Nero is the one burning it all to the ground.

Slowly, my pulse comes back to normal. I wipe away my tears, and straighten up my clothing, turning over every possibility in my mind. I could run. Pack a bag, hit the road. Find another city to get lost in, another shitty job to keep my brother's college tuition paid. Spend every waking minute looking over my shoulder, searching the crowd for a familiar face.

But I already know, it's not an option. Not anymore.

Now that Nero Barretti knows I'm out here, he'll stop at nothing to find me again. He'll hunt me down, no matter what, and he won't care who he has to hurt to get to me.

Teddy.

My brother is safe in college in Indiana, attending lectures and meeting other freshmen at Friday night pizza parties. Oblivious. Happy. I've spent the past ten years raising him, making his life as normal as possible in the wreckage of everything that went down.

He's my reason for everything, and there's nothing I won't do to protect him.

A knock echoes through the apartment.

I flinch.

It comes again, determined.

He's found me.

I get to my feet and take a deep breath. Slide the deadbolt open and throw the door wide.

But it's not Nero on the other side. It's his enforcer, Chase, standing there—with three of his guys, menacing in the dim light. I try not to notice the bloodstains on his shirt, probably the last trace of that drunk guy anyone will ever see.

"Chase," I greet him, pretending it's not a shot of disappointment I feel. "Come in."

He looks surprised, like he was expecting to have to break the door down to get to me.

"Where is he?" I ask. "Where's Nero?"

"He flew back to New York. Business." Chase replies. "He left me to deal with you."

Terror strikes hard, but I hide the shiver. I know how Chase *deals* with people.

Instead, I draw myself up to my full height and give him my most imperious stare. The one I used in my former life, when I was pampered and privileged, and the whole world leapt to give me whatever my heart desired.

When Nero Barretti was the boy I loved, and not the man who wants me dead.

"Take me to him." I say, offering up a final prayer. Because there's only one person who can save me now, and there's no way to run from him. Not anymore. "Take me to the boss."

2

LILY

I DIDN'T EXPECT a first-class ticket, but the drive back to New York is long and humiliating—and gives me plenty of time to wonder if I just made the biggest mistake of my life. Two days tied up in the back of a van, listening to Chase and the other guys speculate over just what Nero will do when we reach the city.

"He's gotta make an example, after what her father did."

"For sure. Everyone's going to know, the Barretti family never forgets. You hear that?" Chase turns and gives me a chilling smile. "Nero's going to have some fun with you."

I don't have to listen in on their conversation. I've spent the past ten years going over every scenario for myself. When your father rats out a Mob boss and gets him locked up in prison, you learn pretty fast that overnight, everything can change.

And just like now, I never saw it coming.

One minute, I was Lily Fordham, pampered daughter, society princess. My life revolved around private school gossip and exclusive parties: art classes and piano lessons and horse-riding at a stable upstate.

The next? My dad was telling me to pack a bag. He'd cut a deal to testify against his boss, Roman Barretti, and we were disappearing into Witness Protection. No more luxurious mansion and credit cards, no more flitting around New York City, no more passionate trysts with the boy I secretly loved. In a heartbeat, I was a thousand miles away, stuck in a modest tract home outside of St. Louis, one of a thousand at my local public school, working weekends at the local Applebee's just to afford community college one day.

New name. New life.

I came back down to earth with a bump, that's for sure.

My little brother was young enough to take it in stride, but my mom didn't make the switch so easily. She'd married a wealthy finance whiz, with country club memberships and an account at Neiman Marcus. This new, modest, anonymous life wasn't part of the deal. It turned out, '*for richer, for poorer*' only went one way. She took off after a couple of years, and we never heard from her again.

Dad's cancer diagnosis came a few years after that, and soon—too soon—it was just me and Teddy.

Now he's all I've got in the world, and I'd do anything to protect him.

Even deliver myself directly into the hands of the new Barretti boss. I figured that with Roman still locked up, Nero would be the man in charge, and it looks like I'm right.

And every mile takes me closer to him.

Every mile brings me nearer to my fate.

I bite back the fear, bitter like metal in my mouth. All I have to go on is that split-second glimpse of him in the alleyway, a moment after a decade of nightmares. I thought I'd figure out a plan on the journey, some way to reason with Nero and get myself out of this mess, but I'm still drawing a blank.

What have you done?

It's too late to turn back now, and I refuse to give Chase the satisfaction of seeing my fear. "I need a bathroom break," I tell him instead.

"You just had one."

"Hours ago. It's that time of the month," I add, lying, just to see him wince.

"Women," he grumbles, but after a few minutes, the van pulls over. The door swings open, and harsh sunlight floods the back of the dark, cramped van.

"Five minutes," Chase warns me, yanking me out. He uncuffs me, hauling me over to the grimy rest stop at the back of the gas station. There are a few cars parked around, and I glimpse the freeway signs nearby. *New York City: 50 miles.*

"Don't try any clever business," he adds, his voice dropping. He glances at the harried looking mom trying to hustle her kids out of the bathroom ahead of me. "I said I'd take you to Nero, but I didn't promise what kind of state you'd be in when you arrive."

I stifle a shiver of fear, remembering the bloodstains on his shirt.

"I'm not stupid," I reply, keeping my voice icy. "Now, can you pick me up a water, or do I have to drink out of the faucet like a dog?"

Chase smirks. "You always were a bitch."

I push open the bathroom door, resisting the urge to slam it in his face. I may be acting high and mighty, but under the surface, I'm scared half to death.

Scared, and running out of time to come up with a plan.

I look around the bathroom. Two stalls, a sink, a window high on the back wall... I could try and squeeze through make a run for it, but I wouldn't get far. Chase isn't dumb—and he's just itching to make a point with me.

Nero's the only one who can save me now.

Save me—or deliver the death sentence for me and my brother.

Moving to the sink, I try my best to clean myself up in the cracked mirror. Two days of gas station junk food and dirty motels haven't been kind, but I smooth down my hair and use paper towels to scrub the dirt off my face. I'm still wearing my hostess outfit from the club, short and tight, with my bra showing through the sheer shirt, but maybe that's for the best.

One chance with Nero, that's all I've got.

And he always did love me in black.

Chase thumps on the bathroom door. "Time to move!"

I take a final breath, and head back outside. This time, he slams the cuffs back on me hard enough to make me yelp, tossing me in the back of the van. I lay there, trying not to cry as we rattle back onto the highway.

You can reason with him, I tell myself. *He loved you, once.*

But what kind of man is he now?

I CAN TELL when we finally reach the city. The sound is unmistakable. Traffic and sirens and that buzz of life. Despite everything, my heart leaps.

God, I missed this place.

I thought about moving back a hundred times, but they were just desperate daydreams. I couldn't risk being spotted; one stray look is all it would take.

But in the end, it turns out nowhere was safe.

We come to a stop, and the van door opens again. We're in some kind of alley, a delivery entrance maybe. I barely have a chance to look around before Chase hauls me to my feet again and roughly wraps some kind of blindfold around my face.

"Seriously?" I ask, as he hustles me straight ahead. I nearly stumble off-balance, but force myself to keep moving. "Is the cloak-and-dagger routine really necessary?"

"Quiet."

"I mean it," I continue, following him blindly. "You think I can't smell the bagels in the air? I bet you a hundred bucks we're within a block of Eddie's. Didn't you guys have a dive bar on 14th Street?"

"I said, shut the hell up!"

The blow lands hard to my stomach, knocking the wind out of me and making me yelp in pain. I stumble back, hitting some solid wall, before I'm yanked forwards again. Inside, the street noise muffled, down a hallway of some kind. Then a door opens, and I'm shoved inside, onto a hard metal chair. "Don't move."

I couldn't, even if I wanted to. It's not just the cuffs biting into my wrists or the blindfold over my eyes. Now that we're finally here, I'm suddenly paralyzed with fear.

Nobody knows that I'm here. Nobody would even know where to look if they noticed I'm gone.

I'm completely at their mercy.

At *his* mercy.

The door slams, and then there's silence. I wait, my heart skittering an anxious rhythm in my chest.

And I wait.

The minutes tick past, or is it hours? I have no idea. I shift, uncomfortable on my chair.

"Hello?" I call. "Anyone there?"

Silence.

I gulp. Maybe they've forgotten about me, or maybe they're all standing around somewhere, laughing at what's become of me. But I refuse to let them see how scared I really am. I yell louder.

"Whatever games you think you're playing, I've had

enough. I get it: You're the powerful one. The big mob boss. So cut the bullshit and show yourself."

Nothing.

"I want to talk to Nero, right now!"

More silence. Then a voice comes, so close it makes me gasp. Inches away, a low, throaty growl that sends shivers down my spine.

Shivers of fear—and desire.

Because I would know that voice anywhere. And he's standing close enough to touch.

"Be careful what you wish for."

3

NERO

LILY FORDHAM.

Fuck.

Of all the ways I imagined us in the same room again, I didn't picture this. Don't get me wrong, the handcuffs and blindfold have made a few appearances in my fantasies, but those were always just that:

Fantasy.

After she left, she damn near drove me crazy, remembering. I couldn't get her out of my mind, burying my cock in some other girl but thinking of Lily the whole time: The way she broke, sobbing with pleasure in my arms. The taste of her mouth, eager and willing.

The breathtaking grip of her slick cunt.

But Lily, here in the flesh after all this time?

Fuck.

I stand in the doorway, just taking in the sight of the woman who's haunted me for the past two days since Vegas— and the past ten years. The blonde hair, tousled around her face. Those lush breasts, spilling over the neckline of her sheer blouse. Legs for days, stretching out from a tight miniskirt all the way down to a pair of kinky black leather sandals I want wrapped around my neck.

When I knew her last, Lily was barely sixteen. Still a girl.

Now, she's all woman.

"Nero?"

She swallows, her breath hitching. Her breasts lift with the motion, tongue wetting her lips, and just like that, I'm hard. Imagining those nipples naked and stiff for me. Feeding every inch of my cock between those sweet lips.

"Nero, I came here to talk."

"Really, princess?" I reply, strolling closer. "I thought you were here because I ordered it so."

She stops, and shivers again. "Can you take this thing off?" she asks, her voice sweet and persuasive. "Come on, Nero. It's not like I haven't seen you before."

Seen me. Betrayed me. *Consumed me.*

I feel the wave of old emotion rise up. I need to get a fucking grip. "You'll do what I say, when I say it," I grind out— and then I walk out, slamming the door behind me with a crash.

Goddammit.

I catch my breath, furious—at myself as much as her. How long has it been since she made a fucking fool of me? Ten long years. I'm not a lovesick kid anymore, I'm a man now.

The man.

And Lily is going to have to realize, she can't sweet-talk me this time around.

I head back to my office and pour myself a drink, trying to think straight. I've gone over it for days, ever since I stumbled over her in that alley in Vegas. I know what's expected of me in this situation. No mercy. No exceptions. But I've got more in play than just an old vendetta, and I need to make sure that nothing screws up my plans.

"What do you think?" Chase saunters in, looking smug. "Like Christmas, all wrapped up with a pretty bow."

I pour him a glass of whiskey too. He's earned it.

"Not such a princess now, is she?" Chase snorts. "Man, I remember how she'd walk around, acting untouchable. Well, she's not so untouchable anymore."

There's something to his sneer than makes me stop. "What did you do?" I demand, lunging for him before I can even think.

"Woah, nothing!" Chase puts up his hands, surprised. "Well, maybe just a little roughing up on the ride. But come on, that club we found her at? Guess Miss Innocent turned out to be nothing but a whore."

I ignore the flare of jealousy. I already overreacted once on her behalf, disposing of that guy in the alleyway. Now I remind myself again, what Lily did, or who she's been doing it with, is none of my concern.

No, the only thing I care about is what she's willing to do right now.

"And her father?"

Chase shakes his head. "She wouldn't give him up. The brother, neither. I didn't go too hard, figured you'd enjoy getting the info out of her."

I nod. "I will."

Chase grins. "People need to know. Doesn't matter if it's been ten years, or a hundred. You cross a fucking Barretti, and we'll find you in the end."

I nod again. I know the code. It runs as deep as blood in our organization. There's no virtue greater than loyalty. And Lily's father sinned worst of all.

"Roman will be pleased," Chase adds, gulping his drink. "Fuck, that family stole his life from him. Ten years locked up—and another ten to go. Death is too kind for a betrayal like that."

Roman. I can just imagine my father when he gets the news

—if his jailhouse whisper network hasn't already told him. Even behind bars, he's feared and respected. And he raised me to be just the same. Brutal. Uncompromising.

Ruthless.

"I'll get the information out of her," I say, finishing my drink. "Her father, her brother, everyone. But nobody touches her aside from me. I mean it," I add, narrowing my eyes. "Spread the word. She's under my protection until the moment I decide it ends."

"Yes, *boss.*" Chase drawls, teasing. We've been friends for as long as I can remember, and I know there's nobody who has my back like him. He winks at me. "Have fun with that."

I scowl. There's nothing fun about dredging up old memories with Lily Fordham, which is why I need to keep my eyes on the prize.

"Is Miles back?" I change the subject, asking about one of my lieutenants, a guy I've tasked with my most *tricky* legal problems.

"Not yet." Chase takes another drink. "I don't know why you're running in circles for this politician. Just stick some cash in a briefcase and the guy will do whatever we want."

I shake my head. "This guy's different. He's not some chump on the liquor board, it's going to take finesse to get him to go along with my plans."

"It's a distraction, that's what it is," Chase says, a note of complaint creeping into his voice. "C'mon, Nero. You've been chasing this deal for way too long. We've got more pressing business on the table. We need to lock down the new import routes out of South America, my guys are working on a connect at the port—"

"And we will." I cut him off. "Or are you saying I can't multitask?"

Chase backs down in a hurry.

"Course not," he says, with a grin. "But all work and no play..."

"I'll play plenty when this deal is all sewn up."

The deal of a lifetime. The one that will take the Barretti organization off the streets—from low-life protection rackets and dealing to a legit, multi-million dollar business enterprise. If I can get this politician to play ball.

"Why not get started early?" Chase grins, nodding to the storeroom where Lily is waiting. "I'm sure she learned plenty of tricks out there in Vegas."

My cock twitches with anticipation at the thought. Whatever she learned, I'm sure as hell going to find out.

Lily Fordham owes me.

And now it's time to collect.

4

LILY

THE BLINDFOLD LIFTS from my eyes, and I blink, adjusting to the light. I'm in a dim storeroom, surrounded by crates of beer and booze, and—

Him.

My heart stops. He's dressed casually in a black shirt and jeans, the cuffs rolled up over muscular forearms, but there's nothing casual about his presence: His broad, looming body radiates tightly wound tension. *Danger.* He's unshaven, his hair is tousled, and his eyes are full of contempt as he looks down at me, bound here at his mercy.

I feel an involuntary shudder, at the awesome strength of masculinity on show. This is not a man to be charmed or reasoned with.

This is a man who rules with an iron fist.

And Lord, is he sexy as hell.

"Well, what do we have here?" Nero drawls, sauntering closer. The light catches on his shoulders, broad and thick.

I force myself not to show fear. "Nero," I say casually, like

I'm bored with all of this. "You took your time. Busy day at the office?"

I catch a flash of a smile, but just as fast, Nero wipes it off his face. His eyes bore into me, steely.

"Careful, princess. You're not in Vegas anymore."

"Clearly," I shoot back. "Although I could use a breakfast buffet right about now. You haven't learned the art of hospitality, I see."

"Oh, I've learned plenty since you saw me last," Nero drawls. "Would you like to find out?"

His gaze trails slowly over every inch of my body, and I swear my thighs clench just remembering his touch. The things he could do to me.

The pleasure he unlocked.

I was sixteen when Nero Barretti took my virginity, and damn him, no man has ever compared.

I swallow hard, fighting the sweaty, sensual memories. That was a lifetime ago. And both Nero and I are different people now.

"Thanks, but I'll pass," I reply, keeping my voice cool. "I doubt I'd be impressed, either way."

Nero narrows his eyes at me. "Enough small talk, princess. There's only one reason why you're still alive right now. Where's your father?" he demands.

"58 Arbor Way, Chesterfield," I reply immediately. "A little town outside St. Louis."

Nero looks surprised thatI would give him up so easily. But what's the use in hiding the truth?

It can't hurt him now.

"Plot eighty-three-five," I continue. "Near the oak tree. He's been rotting there for seven years now, but your minions can dig him up to make sure."

"He's dead? I don't believe you." Nero looks thrown.

I glare at him, feeling the old sting of grief. "If it makes you feel any better, he went slowly. It wasn't pretty, in the end."

Nero pauses. "I'm sorry," he says quietly, like he means it, too.

I snort. "Sorry that you don't get to make a big splash killing him yourself, I'm sure. That's what you want us for, isn't it? To send a message, about the big bad Barretti family who always pay their debts. You might want to watch *Game of Thrones*," I add, unable to help myself. "Didn't work out too well for the Lannisters, and it might not work out for you."

"Is that a threat?" Nero's voice drops. Chillingly calm.

I shiver. "No. Not from me. But guys in your line of work don't last too long. They either wind up dead or in jail."

"And whose fault is that?"

I don't reply, shifting uncomfortably under his stare.

"Where's Teddy?" he asks at last.

I shake my head. "No." I say immediately. "You don't get him."

"You misunderstand me, princess. I get whatever I want."

Nero strolls closer to me and crosses his arms, the casual gesture belying the coiled power of his physique. He looms over me, so close that I can feel the heat radiating off his body.

God, he looks too good.

I gulp, looking away. Trying to find solid ground again, any way to get out of this conversation alive.

Alive, and without the treacherous burn of desire coursing in my bloodstream.

"I came here because I want to make a deal," I say, my voice shaking. "Teddy gets your protection. He stays safe. You leave the both of us alive."

"And what do you have to offer that could possibly be worth that much?" he drawls, amusement in his eyes.

"If I recall, there used to be plenty you wanted. Begged for, even." I cross my legs slowly, my heart in my throat.

Nero's eyes flit lower, but the infuriating smirk remains.

"That was a long time ago, Princess. A man always wants what he can't have, and well... I've had you. The bloom is off the rose."

"You bastard!" I lunge for him without thinking, but he easily holds me back. Gripping my bound wrists with one hand. Making a mockery of my impotent fury.

"I told you, careful." The amusement is gone from his eyes, and only controlled fury remains. "My patience is wearing thin. And if you can't tell me what I want to know, then I'll have no use for you."

I fight to stay calm.

"Do what you will with me." I say, holding back tears. "But I won't give up Teddy. No matter what."

Nero studies me for a long moment. Then he turns to walk out.

"Wait!" I blurt, panicking. "Please... He's just a kid. He didn't know anything! You have to leave him alone. *Please!*"

He pauses. "I wonder... Just what will you do to protect him?"

My voice falters, but I don't flinch. "Anything. I'll do anything you want."

Nero meets my eyes, inscrutable.

Unmovable.

"Well, princess... I'm going to hold you to that."

I open my mouth to ask what he means by that, but before I get the words out, Nero pulls the blindfold back over my head. I don't have a smart retort this time as I'm led blindly from the room. My fear is starting to take hold, which it the last thing I need in a situation like this.

Things aren't going well. My plan to talk my way out of this has failed spectacularly, and I can't ignore the unease creeping down my spine. I had put all my eggs in one basket, planning to appeal to the soft side of Nero, but he clearly doesn't have one. This man is a stranger to me now, cold and dangerous.

I'm so screwed.

I'm put into a vehicle, but it's not the same van that brought me here. My wrists are still cuffed behind my back, and my aching arms press against cool leather. When the engine starts, the sound is a soft purr, and the ride is smooth. The driver doesn't speak, but a sixth sense tells me that Nero is nearby.

I can feel him now, his presence. An invisible force making every nerve in my body alert, waiting for his next move.

Whatever that move may be.

My mind races. Is there anything I can do or say to keep Teddy safe? There's probably no hope for me, but damn it, I'm not going to let them get to my brother.

My sense of time is distorted by my lack of sight and rising apprehension, but I don't think we've been driving for long when we come to a stop. The blindfold shifts as I'm pulled from the car, and I get a quick view of a parking garage before it's adjusted again.

"This is getting old," I say out loud, clinging to the exasperation I feel. Much better than fear and dread. "All this subterfuge, and for what? You've already made it clear, there's nowhere for me to run to."

But there's silence, of course.

One short elevator ride later, we seem to reach our destination. Someone uncuffs me, and whips off the blindfold again.

"Finally," I sigh, rubbing my wrists, as I look around. I'm in the middle of a huge bedroom suite. The furniture is grey and black, very masculine, with the only pop of color coming from the abstract art on the walls. There's nothing personal in my eyesight, but the place screams Nero. This has to be his place.

I shiver. As intimidating as the bare office room was, this is daunting in a whole other way. The huge, king-sized bed....

Why am I here?

"Do the amenities meet your standards, Princess?"

I spin around. Nero is in the doorway, watching me. "What's going on?" I ask, trying to keep the fear from my voice. "Where am I?"

"Where I want you to be." Nero scowls. "You'll stay here, where I can keep an eye on you."

"So, I'm your prisoner," I say, that knot of fear turning to lead in my stomach.

He strolls closer. "You're the one who asked to be brought to me, Princess. I could have left you in Vegas."

"Still breathing?" I retort.

He tilts his head. "Now, that's the question, isn't it?"

I swallow hard, uncomfortable under his dark-eyed scrutiny. The feel of his eyes on me prickles at my skin, making my heart race.

Then suddenly, Nero's gaze darkens. He lunges forwards and yanks at the neckline of my top, pulling it aside. I let out a yelp of shock and fear—but Nero isn't touching me, he's staring at my shoulder.

"Who did this to you?" he growls, his whole body coiled with fury.

I gape in confusion—and then catch a sight of my reflection in the mirror on the bureau. A purple bruise is blooming across my skin, raw and ugly.

"Was this Chase?" Nero demands, eyes blazing. "If one of his guys laid a hand on you—"

"You'll do what?" I shoot back, pulling away and yanking my top up again. "Give him a prize?"

Hurt flashes in Nero's gaze, but it's gone so fast, I must have been imagining it. "Tell me who did it," he growls, stepping close again, towering over me, so he's all I can see.

All I can feel.

"It was the guy in Vegas," I blurt, overwhelmed by his presence. "The one you..."

I trail off, remembering the bloodstains on Chase's clothes.

The one he killed.

Nero seems to relax at my words. He reaches out again, gentle this time, and softly touches the bruised skin. "Does it hurt?"

The concern in his voice takes me by surprise. I swallow again, losing grip on my anger. I shake my head. "It's fine now," I whisper, shivering at his touch.

Our eyes lock, and it's like the years fall away. He's not my cruel captor, and I'm not desperate to stay alive. We're just... Us. Drawn together with the same magnetic connection that had me breaking all the rules, and him risking his father's wrath. Young, and reckless, and so deep in love, I never wanted to come up for air.

Nero's hand traces higher, up to my jaw, and over my cheek. "You got freckles," he murmurs, his voice rough and hoarse as he softly strokes over them.

I shiver, hypnotized. "The sun... out West."

His thumb reaches my lips, and he rubs it over them, back and forth. I inhale in a rush, awareness flooding through me. Swaying closer. Eyes locked on his as he slips his thumb between my lips and sinks it inside my mouth.

Holy heaven.

I shudder at the sensual intrusion, parting my lips wider.

And then I suck.

Nero's eyes flare with lust, and he sounds a low, ragged groan. The sound ricochets through my body, making my nipples tighten and every nerve ending flare to life.

Desire... Fuck, I've barely felt a flicker in years, and now it's hitting me like a damn avalanche. Blotting out everything but Nero, and his labored breath, and the raw, animal passion in his eyes.

Suddenly, noise comes from down the hallway. "Boss?" a voice calls. Chase, I think.

Nero seems to remember himself. He snatches his hand away, cursing under his breath.

I reel back, stunned. "Nero..." I blurt, but he's already striding to the door, the spell broken.

"Clean yourself up." He says harshly, shooting me a dismissive glance. "You look a mess. And you smell even worse."

He's gone before I can respond. Heat flushes my cheeks at his cold insult—even as my body aches from his gentle caress.

What the hell just happened?

I take a deep breath, half-tempted to stay in my filthy, sweaty clothes just to spite him. Then I see a door ajar to the bathroom: It's spotless marble, and might be bigger than my apartment back in Vegas.

God, I could use a shower.

In the war between comfort and spite, comfort wins. I don't waste time before stripping and stepping into the shower, not sure when Nero will come back for me or what he has planned. The hot water feels heavenly against my skin, and I let out a small sigh. There's a row of expensive toiletries waiting on the ledge, so I lather up, scrubbing every inch of grime off my body and washing my hair. I take my time, trying to delay the inevitable. But I know, it's useless. Nero doesn't wait for anyone.

Nero...

I exhale a shaky breath, still reeling from seeing him again. From *wanting* him again.

It's crazy, to be turned on in the midst of all this fear and mayhem, but I can't help it. Like an automatic chemical reaction, just the sight of him—the scent of him—sends my hormones screaming to life, flooding my body with pure aching lust. I can't help remembering the way his body felt against me all *inside me*, that thick, sweet drive that sent me to heaven and back.

Nobody learned my body the way he did. Nobody gave me pleasure like him.

But he'd been gentle, too, when we were together. So careful not to hurt me, so eager to please. I'd only seen glimpses of his power, his dominance—and oh, how they thrilled me.

What would it feel like now that dominance was in full flight?

He wouldn't make love to me tenderly now, that much I know. No, Nero would hold me down and fuck me to the hilt. Roughly. Angrily. He'd demand my surrender—and then punish me if I tried to deny him.

My pussy clenches at the thought, and my blood runs hotter, imagining his rough hands holding me down. Those broad shoulders pinning me beneath him.

That cruel mouth hissing dark, dirty orders.

Orders I would only be too happy to obey...

Fuck. No. Bad Lily.

I try to remind myself that he's a terrible, dangerous man, but it doesn't help. That risky edge makes my heart race as I straddle the then line between desire and fear.

Damn it, Lily. Focus on what's important.

Is Nero really considering sparing Teddy? I meant it when I said that I'd do anything, but I can't help worrying about what he'll ask of me.

Men like Nero have no limits.

. . .

WHEN I FINALLY GET OUT OF the shower, I feel somewhat human again. I step back into the bedroom with a towel wrapped around my body and find that somebody's been there: Clothes are waiting, laid out on the bed.

I move closer. There's tasteful lingerie, and a breezy designer sundress with a daisy print on it, the kind of thing I would have worn in my old life. Silk, lace, sophistication... The style of clothes I haven't been able to afford in, well, ever. Nostalgia washes over me as I pull it on, tightening the belt around my waist. There are even strappy sandals in a matching yellow, the sizing all perfect. Looking in the mirror, it's like staring at a ghost:

Lily Fordham, designer debutante.

Is this who Nero thinks I still am?

I decide that I'm not waiting around for him, so I pull my damp hair into a loose braid and venture out of the bedroom. The hallway opens up, and I find myself standing in a huge loft space. The apartment is massive, taking over what must be a full floor with industrial-chic vibes: High ceilings, exposed brick, and tall windows that show a fantastic view of the city.

I pause, thrown. The place is stylish and masculine, and clearly expensive, but what was I expecting? The Barretti family has made a fortune from their criminal empire, and Nero is the heir to everything. Of course he's living in luxury.

Luxury bought in blood.

I hear voices and walk toward them, passing the open kitchen and living room space until I reach a door that's been left ajar. I know I'm pushing my luck, but I press my face close and peer inside.

It's an office, with a huge glass desk and walls of bookcases. Nero is lounging behind the desk, talking to two other men and a woman. I recognize Chase, of course, and the woman, Avery.

She's about my age and was raised in the Barretti organization. She sits, expression alert as the other man speaks.

"It's not going to be easy," he's saying. He has brown hair, and a serious look about him, wearing a pair of glasses as he consults a yellow legal pad. "McKenna's people keep refusing a meeting."

"You told them what it was for?" Nero asks.

"I said we were interested in donating to his campaign, discussing his reelection efforts, everything," the man says. "But no luck. He's blowing us off."

"*Me*, you mean," Nero rakes a hand through his hair, looking pissed. "Since when do politicians have standards?"

Politicians? I put two and two together, and figure he must be talking about Ian McKenna, a rising star in the New York political scene. I've seen articles about him in the papers, but what does Nero want with him?

"Miles could try again," Avery offers. "Try some kind of charity approach. Maybe set up a dummy corporation to put some distance between you."

Nero shakes his head. "I don't want distance. I need to get in the same room as the man.

The future of the organization depends on his vote."

Chase shrugs, seeming unconcerned. "Don't worry about it. Everyone has their price. We'll get him."

I can't help but chuckle at that.

All eyes turn to the door. *Busted.* I try to pretend I'm unphased as Nero's eyes rake over me. I want some reaction to my new outfit, but I don't get one.

"What's so funny?" he demands.

"You're talking about Ian McKenna, right?" I ask, and he just gives a curt nod in response. "That guy won't touch your money."

"Why the hell not?" Nero's voice is defensive, as if I've

offended him. "He's too pure? He's a goddamn politician. They're all the same."

"Perhaps," I give a shrug. "Chase was right—for a change. They all have a price. But not in the same way. And Ian McKenna wouldn't care less about a briefcase of your dirty cash, that's not how you can buy him."

Nero narrows his eyes at me. "Explain."

My pulse kicks. He's interested. Curious. And every moment he's listening to what I have to say, he's not thinking about how my family betrayed him.

"Did you do a moment of research on this guy?" I ask, looking around the room.

"Of course," the serious guy—Miles—protests. "I looked into his background, policy goals—"

"But did you look at the PR?" I cut him off. "The guy posed for a two-page spread in *People* magazine with his wife and dog. He's working on a book. He went on Oprah, for God's sake."

"So?" Nero looks blank.

"So, you don't do that if you're staying pushing papers on City Council," I explain. "The guy clearly has ambitions for higher office. Mayor, senate, maybe Governor one day. Which means more scrutiny, security vetting, reporters digging up every dark secret he's got. Any cash he takes now is going to haunt him down the road. A man with ambition like that? He won't risk being associated with the likes of *you*."

A muscle spasms in Nero's jaw as I say those words, and my heart sinks. I'm pretty sure I just screwed up. Why did I have to let my mouth run away with me like that?

I brace myself to get dragged out of here, but instead, Nero's lips curl in a dangerous smile.

I shiver.

"You seem to know a lot about the guy," he says, wheels clearly turning in his mind.

I give what I hope is a careless shrug. "I read the tabloids, that's all."

"Oh, I think you're smarter than that." Nero's voice is silky. Dangerous. "So smart, you can figure out a way to get me in a room with McKenna."

"What?" I gulp. "Me?"

"Yes, you." Nero states. "Tonight."

"But—" I start to protest, but he silences me with a look.

"I'd think very hard before arguing, Princess. You'll make this happen, alright. Your future depends on it."

5

LILY

IF I THOUGHT I knew how things would go with Nero, I could never have expected this: Just a few hours later, I find myself in the back of a limousine wearing a gorgeous gown, deep red with a split up the side to my thigh and classy black stiletto heels. I've covered my bruise in makeup, and there are real diamonds hanging around my neck and from my earlobes. But they may as well have been handcuffs, because I'm still a prisoner of the man sitting beside me.

Nero.

He's looking devastatingly hot in a tuxedo, typing away on his cell phone. I assume he's conducting business—or he's using it as a way to ignore me, because he hasn't said a word to me since he got in the car, leaving me on edge.

I try to steady my nerves. Just because he's keeping me off-balance, impossible to predict his next move, it doesn't mean that I don't have any power here.

I cross my legs, bare thigh flashing through the tasteful slit in my gown and see his jaw clench.

I hide a smile. At least he's still affected by me in *one* way.

I know I should shut the hell up, and plot my next move, but I can't stifle my own curiosity about tonight. Nero in a tuxedo, attending some fancy event—and bringing me along, too? I have to wonder what the hell I've set myself up for here. I told Nero I'd do anything to save Teddy—and I meant it—but it's impossible not to be anxious while I wait for him to fill me in on what exactly is expected of me. All I know so far is that we are headed to a charity event, but he hasn't shared anything more than that.

As the city lights blur outside the limo windows, I finally sigh. "Are you going to tell me anything about this event? Like what your business is with McKenna."

"That's not your concern." He doesn't even look up from his phone.

"Since I'm the one dressed in stilettos and a lace thong, it is."

His jaw clenches again at the mention of my underwear. "Careful, Princess," Nero shoots me a slow, steely look. "Keep running your mouth, and I'll give you something better to do with it."

I inhale in a rush, desire hitting me like a Mack Truck all over again. I fight to hide my reaction. "If you won't tell me what you want, how am I supposed to give it to you?"

Nero's gaze darkens at my inadvertent double entendre. "What I want?" he echoes, his gaze stripping me bare.

I blush. "I meant, out of tonight. From this McKenna guy."

Nero smirks at my reaction. "Why don't you just focus on what's important right now, Princess."

"Which is?"

"Being more useful to me alive than dead."

I shiver, and not with lust this time. I nod and turn away. I can't forget for a moment the threat that he's holding over me, however much my body wants to ignore it. So, I stare out of the window instead, watching as we head to the Upper East Side, arriving in front of a tall, stately building. The limo driver opens my door and I step out, followed by Nero. I look around. I haven't been in this section of town in a long time. Luxurious townhomes and pre-war apartments with a view of Central Park....

"Homesick, Princess?" Nero's voice cuts through my thoughts.

"No," I retort, collecting myself. "Just wondering what brings you so far out of your league."

Nero's eyes flash angrily, but the doorman is already greeting us. As we head inside the building, I notice a bronze plaque bolted to the white brick exterior just beside the door. It says that this place was built in 1891 to serve as a gentlemen's club for New York's most elite; members of the highest social class.

Again, I wonder why Nero has made the trip uptown. Mixing with rich kids was never his style, he liked to brawl in the muck, not sit around chatting about lacrosse and brandy.

Whatever he wants, he must want it *bad*.

As we step inside, I'm immediately in awe. There's a marble floor beneath our feet and a priceless art on the walls. The high ceiling is arched, and there's a grand staircase directly ahead.

"Hello, are you here for the gala?"

I turn my head to see a man standing near the entrance with an iPad in his hand. I didn't even notice him at first as I soaked in my surroundings.

"Yeah." Nero seems almost irritated with the question, and I'm not sure why. "I'm on the list. Nero Barretti."

There's a defiance in his eyes, as if he's daring the man to say he's not allowed here. That defensive attitude won't get him far with the kind of people that we are bound to run into here, but I don't say a word.

"Ah, yes," the man says after scrolling through his iPad. "Welcome, Mr. Barretti." His voice lingers on the name, just this side of a sneer. "How *nice* you could join us. You're just in time for the cocktail reception."

He leads us down a long hallway, to a chic entertaining room. There are a hundred people dressed up just like us, milling around with champagne and canapés. I spot McKenna in the corner, surrounded by a crowd, and my suspicions are confirmed.

This is all about the politician.

Everyone seems to have a drink in their hand, so when a waiter approaches, I order a martini.

"I'm fine," Nero growls, but I shake my head.

"He'll have a scotch, thank you." I tell the waiter with a smile, and he hurries off to the bar to get our drinks.

"What was that?" Nero demands.

I sigh. "Trust me, you'll stick out like a sore thumb if you're the only man here without a strong drink in his hand. It's a cocktail hour. Just hold the thing if you don't want to drink it."

He frowns at me.

"But I'd drink it," I can't help adding. "You need something to loosen you up."

He doesn't argue, and I take the win.

"What's this gala for, anyway?" I ask as the waiter weaves his way through the crowd, headed back toward us.

"Some charity that helps the homeless." Nero shrugs. "I made a donation and got on the guest list."

Of course, he did. Because a guy like Nero isn't getting in any other way. He doesn't belong here.

But I do.

I used to be a part of this world. Used to mingle with people like this all the time, at events with my parents, and all my private school friends. Charity functions, the theater, garden parties, and summers on Cape Cod. It was the life I was raised to,

And just like that, I realize, I do have something of value to Nero. More than just my body, anyway.

I have my charm.

My smile, my small talk, my ability to walk into a room and *belong*. Sure, those skills are rusty as hell, I haven't needed them in ten years, but that social butterfly is still buried deep inside me.

And maybe she's my ticket to safety. If not for me, then my brother, at least.

So if Nero wants to cozy up to McKenna, I need to make it happen.

I take a deep breath, and look around the room again, paying more attention this time. Nero's already drawing curious stares, so I slide my arm through his elbow and lean in closer, acting like a couple.

Nero stiffens at my touch, but I ignore him as I flash a smile at a woman I recognize. She's a trophy wife who loves throwing parties with her banker husband's money. Her daughter was a couple of years below me in school, and thanks to what I'm guessing is the best plastic surgery money can buy, Bitsy Janssen hasn't aged a day since I saw her last.

"Lily Fordham, is that you?" Bitsy exclaims as she reaches me.

"Mrs Janssen, hi!" I squeal, adopting an enthusiastic voice. I air-kiss her on both cheeks. "Look at you, you look incredible."

"All thanks to Doctor Feldman," she coos. "Let me know if you want his number. He's a wizard with Botox."

There's a disdainful snort beside us. Nero.

Bitsy's smile fades as she moves to him. "I'm sorry, I don't believe we've been introduced."

"This is my friend, Nero Barretti." I say quickly.

I see a flicker of recognition in her eyes as I say his name. *Fuck.* But there's no way around it, and thankfully, Bitsy is too polite to mention his career as a Mob boss. "Oh. Well. Lovely to meet you," she says faintly, offering her hand to shake.

Nero scowls at her, not offering her hand. Not even saying a word.

Was the man raised in a barn?

Nope, just the mean streets of the New York underworld.

Quickly, I move between them. "Tell Nina I'd love to catch up," I say with a big smile, trying to cover Nero's faux pas. "It was so good to see you!"

"Likewise," Bitsy says slowly, looking back and forth between Nero and me. She's clearly wondering what the hell I'm doing here with a guy like that.

I wonder what she'd say if she knew the truth.

I steer Nero away before he can insult her anymore. "What is wrong with you?" I whisper, as soon as we're a safe distance away. "I thought you wanted to schmooze with these people."

"And make bullshit small talk?" Nero asks, looking grim. "No thanks. Get me close to McKenna, so we can get the fuck out of here."

I fight to hide my frustration. "You've already tried a direct approach, and it failed, so this time, you need an introduction from someone he respects. So, you blend, you mingle, you make *bullshit small-talk*, and then—only then—do we get someone to take us to McKenna. You brought me here for a reason," I add. "So trust me on this, OK?"

Nero doesn't look happy, but he drains his whiskey, and gives a sharp nod. "Fine. But I draw the fucking line at air-kisses."

"The women of the Upper East Side will weep," I remark dryly, and tow him back into the fray.

This time, at least, he doesn't laugh in anyone's face. Nero doesn't say much as we stop and chat with various people, but I compensate for it by bringing all my charm, cooing over dresses, and summer house plans, and a darling new exhibit at the Met. But I know what I'm doing, and soon enough, I maneuver us into a conversation with a couple who are big on the political scene, discussing various charity efforts.

When the chat lulls, I look around. "Is that Ian McKenna?" I ask, pretending to be surprised.

The wife turns. "Oh yes, he's so generous with his time for a good cause."

"I'm a big admirer," I say, "His proposals for dealing with homelessness are so smart."

"Then I must introduce you!" she exclaims. "Ian, darling, come meet my new friends." She beckons him over, and she must have donated generously to his campaign, because Ian comes right away, greeting us with a smile.

"Any friend of Susie's is a friend of mine," he says. "A pleasure to meet you...?"

"Lily Fordham," I smile, feeling victorious.

"It's nice to meet you Miss Fordham," he says. He's tall and good-looking in a preppy way, his smile showing off perfectly straight, white teeth. It's the kind of smile that will look good on a banner next to the words *McKenna for Congress*. "This is my wife, Fiona."

"Lovely to meet you." I say. She's beautiful in a polished sort of way, with flawless hair and makeup, and a kind expression as she greets us.

I'm about to introduce Nero when he speaks up.

"I'm Nero Barretti. I've been trying to schedule a meeting with you, but your people won't allow it to happen."

The aggressive tone of his voice makes me flinch. Has he not listened to a single word I've said all night?

McKenna's polite smile doesn't even falter. "Ah, well, I'm sorry to hear that we haven't been able to arrange it. My schedule is hard to manage, and I'm just thankful that I have others to do it for me. Fiona will tell you, I can't keep the days of the week straight!"

Everyone laughs along—except Nero.

"If you have time for a party, then you can have a conversation with me," Nero says, and I can tell by the coldness in his voice that he's trying to intimidate McKenna.

Fuck. I squeeze his arm, trying to signal him to back off. He's ruining everything.

This is a different world than the one he's used to. The rules that make him a king don't apply here.

McKenna's smile slips. "As I said, my schedule is full, Mr. Barretti."

"Full, with all your important work," I blurt loudly. "So we won't keep you. Thank you for your time." I pull on Nero's arm. "Let's grab another drink before they start the speeches." I look at McKenna's wife and roll my eyes even as a smile stretches across my face. "They love to drag out the speeches, don't they?"

She laughs politely. "That's a good point, this one can listen to himself talk all night."

Everyone chuckles again, hopefully glossing over the damage of Nero's rudeness.

"See you soon," I add, steering Nero away. Sure enough, someone taps a glass for silence and takes to the stage area to start speaking, but I don't stop until Nero and I are through a pair of French doors into the courtyard, out of earshot of the crowd.

"What the fuck was that?" Nero demands, yanking away

from me the minute we're clear. "I spent all night waiting to talk to the guy, and the minute we get close, you pull me away?"

"You were coming on too strong." I tell him. "Bringing up business in the first conversation? That's not how things are done."

Nero scowls. "Yeah, well I do things differently."

"Which is why you haven't gotten anywhere," I remind him. "Look around. No one is here to discuss business. This kind of thing isn't about the fancy clothes or the booze or even the charity. It's about forming connections that you can utilize later. This is a different game to the one you've been playing, and you have to know the rules, or you're just wasting your time."

Nero snorts. "I guess you'd know all about playing games, wouldn't you, Princess?"

I flinch at the coldness in his eyes.

"Can you try not to insult anyone for the next five minutes?" I ask. I start moving away, but his fingers close around my wrist.

"Where are you going?"

His grip burns me. I take a deep breath. "The bathroom." I point with a raised eyebrow. "Unless you plan to make me hold it all night long?"

"Come right back."

"Don't be so needy," I can't help teasing, then duck away before he can reply.

I know that I'm pushing him, but I can't seem to help myself. He's under my skin, and I need to hide that from him. It's the only way to hold onto a shred of my pride.

I head to the bathroom, pushing through the door to find myself in a women's lounge. There are dusky rose couches and chairs, a full sitting area complete with ornate vanity mirrors along the wall. A vase of fresh-cut flowers sits on the counter, and I breathe in the sweetness of them.

So feminine. So over-the-top.

The actual bathrooms are just beyond the lounge, four private stalls with sink and toilet. But I don't go in there. I don't really need to. I just want a moment to myself.

To get a hold of the emotions whirling in my chest.

Being here is throwing me for a loop. I'm getting a glimpse of the life I was supposed to be living this whole time. I was groomed to fit in with these high-society types, to be one of them. A life of luxury and ease.

After my family fled into Witness Protection, I didn't let myself think about everything that had been taken from me. Why bother when it wouldn't change my circumstances?

But there's no avoiding what I lost now. It's being thrown in my face.

Who would I be without the Barrettis burning my family to the ground?

I take a deep breath and try to pull myself together. Looking in the mirror, I barely recognize myself. This isn't the waitress at the shitty strip club staring back at me.

I'm a princess tonight.

The door opens, and two women enter. Fiona McKenna, and another familiar face. It's Marissa Chambers, an friend from school. She comes from old money, born with a silver spoon in her mouth, but she was always nice and a fun time.

"It's a disaster," Marissa is saying, not noticing me yet. "My colorist moved to L.A. to work on the hair of actresses on movie sets or something like that, and I haven't been able to find anyone that knows what they're doing since."

"You poor thing," Fiona replies. "It can be a nightmare to find someone you can trust. It took me years before I finally discovered Gloria. She works at *Marche* salon on Fifth—"

"Lily?" Marissa interrupts Fiona as she spots me, and I try to look surprised, as if I wasn't just eavesdropping.

"Marissa? Is that you?"

Marissa lets out a squeal and dives in for a genuine hug. Fiona is called away, and I silently curse at the missed opportunity to get to know her. She could definitely be a path in with her husband.

"It's been so long!" Marissa says, her enthusiasm infectious.

"It really has." I smile back, my first genuine smile of the night. "How have you been?"

"Well..." she holds up her left hand, letting out a squeal as she shows off a huge engagement ring and wedding band. The diamond even reflects light.

"Wow. Congratulations! Who's the lucky guy?"

"His name is Ryan. His family owns the largest vineyard in Napa Valley, and he adores me." She laughs. "So, what have you been up to? You just up and disappeared on us."

"I know..." I cast my mind out for a good lie. I should have thought of this before. I really wasn't thinking about running into anyone I know. "I'm sure you know what it's like when you get the urge to travel. I've spent most of my time in Europe."

"Amazing," she says with a sigh. "Art school, right? Did you find inspiration in Europe?"

Her question is a punch to the gut. My dreams of having an art career died the minute I left town.

"Of course," I say, making sure that my voice doesn't convey the way I feel inside. "But I've just been really focused on my charity work for the last few years."

"We must have lunch," Marissa insists. "I want to hear everything!"

"Totally," I lie, before saying goodbye and exiting the bathroom. I hurry back to the ballroom, sure Nero's wondering what's taking me so long.

But I'm wrong. Why would he think about me at all when there's a gorgeous blonde throwing herself at him?

I watch from a distance, as the woman reaches out to caress his arm while they're talking. His eyes are glued to her, and she keeps tossing her hair in a coquettish way while leaning her lithe body his way.

It's clear that she wants him, and I tell myself that I don't care.

But that's a lie. In just the few short hours that I've been around him, my old desire has reignited, despite the fact that he hates me now. I want to ignore this sickening jealousy that I feel, but I don't think I can.

Coming back to New York, trying to make some deal with Nero... It was a mistake. I can't think clearly when I still want him like this. Right now, life on the run feels safer than dealing with my feelings for him.

That's when it hits me.

He's not paying attention to where I am. For the first time in days, nobody is. No armed guards. No handcuffs.

I have a chance to get away.

Looking around, I see swinging doors that lead to the kitchen nearby. Before I can think twice, I walk through them, quickly passing chefs and the bustle of activity as I head to a back entrance. The breeze is cool on my bare arms as I step outside—and keep walking.

Towards freedom.

6

LILY

AS SOON AS I get outside, I run. Even in my heels, I'm able to move at a fast clip for three blocks before my feet are aching and there's a stitch in my side.

This is what I get for skipping the gym.

I don't know what to do now. I didn't think this through. I have no money, no place to stay, and I'm wearing a fancy-ass cocktail dress and heels. I don't even have a cell phone.

But I've committed to running away now.

So, I keep to the shadows as best as I can, trying not to draw too much attention to myself. Soon, the streets blur, and I lose track of the neighborhood. The buildings turn industrial, the further I head away from the ritzy party address, and there are fewer people on the streets.

What have I done?

With every block, my panic grows. Nero is definitely going to come after me, and he'll be furious if he finds me.

If.

All I can do is hope I stay one step ahead. I have a head start, after all; maybe five minutes before he figures I'm gone—more if that blonde he was flirting with keeps him occupied. Besides, how will he find me? It's a big city, and even I don't know where I'm heading, so I can't see how he'd be able to track me down.

Still, my fear is working against me. My footsteps slow, stumbling in my heels, and I find myself flinching at every passing car and shadow. I can't shake the certainty that my impulsive decision to flee is going to get me killed.

Where do I go from here?

"Well, well, well... What do we have here?"

The voice seemed to come out of nowhere and I stop in my tracks. Another stupid move.

I'm beside a dark alley and as I look around, two men emerge from the shadows. I know now that I should have run as soon as I heard someone speak, but it's too late. They stroll closer, blocking me in on either side.

"You lost, sweetheart?" One asks, his eyes raking over me.

"Course she's lost," the other replies, before I can say anything. "Fancy lady like this, all on her own. Where're you heading? We'll set you in the right direction."

I swallow hard, painfully aware of my plunging gown and the diamonds at my throat. Why didn't I grab a coat on the way out? I'm practically screaming 'easy target' here.

"Thanks, but I'm fine," I lie, edging backwards. "I'm meeting some friends."

"Oh yeah?" one of the guys moves closer. "Are they as pretty as you?"

My pulse kicks with fear. "I really should be going," I try to sound firm. "Goodnight."

I try to walk past them, but they move to block my path.

"Aww, what's the hurry?" One of them reaches out and touches the diamonds at my neck. I recoil from the feel of his fingers on my neck, and his smile drops. "Too good to be seen with us, is that it?"

"N—no..."

My heart pounds against my ribcage as I back up until I collide with a brick wall. The faint white illumination coming from a streetlight at the end of the alley is just enough to let me see the wicked intent on their faces.

I think fast. "You can have the necklace," I blurt, reaching to fumble with the clasp. "Please, I just need to go,"

They exchange a chuckle. "That's mighty generous, sweetheart. But I think you've got some other goodies worth trying on for size."

He reaches for me again, but suddenly, we're all bathed in bright light. I turn my head to see the limousine pull to a stop, its headlights shining on us, blinding me.

Nero gets out.

I exhale in a whoosh, relief washing over me. Because faced with a choice between the devil I know and the one I don't, I'll take the devil in a formal tux any day.

Even if he's walking towards us with murder in his eyes.

Nero comes to a stop twenty paces away and casually puts his hands in his pockets as he stares them both down. "You have your hands on my property."

One of the guys snorts. "So what?"

Nero takes another step, so the man can see his face. And whatever emotion is written there, it's enough to make even these two meatheads reconsider.

"Fuck it," one mutters. "She's not worth the trouble."

They move away from me, but Nero stops the guy who was grabbing me. "I said, you touched what doesn't belong to me."

He gulps. "I'm sorry, man."

"I'm sure you will be."

He moves so fast, nobody sees it coming. With a swift twist

and a snap of his arm, the guy is on the ground, crying out in pain. Nero lifts on foot and brings it down so hard on the guy's hand, I hear the bones break.

What the hell? I gape at the sudden, ruthless violence, but Nero looks entirely unconcerned. "Now, fuck off," he growls at the guy, who is nursing his shattered hand.

He's still sobbing when his friend drags him up and away, out of sight around the corner.

I have to admit, a part of me is relieved to see them go. Then Nero shifts his attention to me. The cold look in his eyes makes me shudder, and I know that I'm not any safer because of his arrival.

Out of the frying pan... and into the burning pit of hell.

I try to collect myself. "How did you find me?" I ask, straightening up.

I have to know. It seems impossible that he came upon this scene by chance.

"You think I don't know that you're a flight risk?" Nero asks.

"Do you blame me?" I shoot back, my anger rising in the face of his disdain. "You haven't exactly given me the warmest welcome."

"So obviously, you try and go get yourself killed. Or worse." He beckons, looking impatient. I shake my head stubbornly. His eyes narrow as he grabs my arm and yanks me towards the limo. "You should be thanking me, princess. You're just lucky that I put that tracking device in your necklace. Because if I hadn't come along when I did..."

He's right, but his words still burn.

"*Lucky?*" I repeat, my voice rising with emotion. "*Lucky* is the last thing I am. You've destroyed my life, Nero Barretti. I wish I'd never even met you!"

My voice echoes in the dark night. He opens his mouth to

respond, but I don't wait for him to answer. I jab a finger in his face, fury hot in my veins.

"I'll never forgive you for this. For dragging me back to the city. For taking me hostage. For threatening Teddy. You're a monster, and I hate you! I hate you!"

In an instant, Nero backs me up against the car, his face just inches from mine. His body pressed hot and hard against me.

I gasp, suddenly overwhelmed by his presence, taut muscle crushing me against the hard metal. "You hate me, Princess?" he asks in a low, dangerous voice.

I nod, not trusting myself to speak. Not with the scent of him slipping through my system. Not with desire pulsing hard between my thighs.

But Nero can see through me. he always did.

His lips curl in a slow smirk. "It doesn't feel that way to me."

He's kissing me before I even realize what's happening, his mouth slamming hard against mine as he grips my jaw tightly in his hands. It's cruel, dominant kiss, almost like a punishment, but even as my mind reels, my body knows exactly what to do.

Surrender...

I mold my lips to his, moaning as his tongue plunges inside, claiming my mouth. Heat crackles through me, fire in my veins as my body comes screaming to life under his cruel, demanding touch. God, it's just as hot as I remember, and I'm flooded with feelings that should be long dead.

Feelings that are going to destroy me.

I'm still lost in the blazing inferno of the kiss when Nero yanks away. I feel ashamed when I see the lack of emotion in his eyes.

"Let this be a lesson for you," he says grimly, releasing me. "The next time you run, you won't live to see dawn."

. . .

THE RIDE back to his place is heavy with silence as before, but it doesn't bother me this time. I'm too busy thinking about my impossible situation.

Right now, I'm a dead woman walking. By all the mafia rules, I should already be bleeding in a gutter somewhere. My father betrayed the Barrettis, and that's a debt that needs to be repaid—not just as revenge against my family, but as a message to everyone else:

'Fuck with the Barrettis and suffer the consequences.'

I thought I could reason with Nero, charm him into letting me and my brother go. But clearly, that plan isn't going to work.

So, I need a new plan. One that keeps me breathing—and protects my brother, too.

But how?

The city blurs outside the windows as I turn over every possibility in my mind. I need to be smart if I'm going to get out of this mess. Flying by the seat of my pants isn't cutting it, as tonight proved beyond a doubt. Being reckless and impulsive won't help me get away from Nero, and besides, even if I do escape him again, where would I go? I need money, a safe place to hide, friends to help me...

And I have precisely none of the above.

There's no escaping it: For now, I'm a prisoner. *His* prisoner. And if I'm going to walk away from my captivity, I need to do it with Nero's blessing.

Because I know in my bones, if I run again... He would never stop hunting me.

So how can I convince him to let me go? To even keep me alive another day long enough to think about it?

"Out."

I look up to find we're back at his place, in a parking garage.

I get out of the limo and follow him upstairs to his loft. I don't have handcuffs binding my wrists anymore, but we both know that I don't need them.

I don't have a choice but to stay.

Nero leads me back to the same bedroom I was in beforehand. "This will be yours," he says in a curt voice. His face is expressionless. "If there's shit you need, make a list. Someone will get it for you."

"How long am I staying?" I ask, looking around with new eyes.

"Until I decide you're done here."

"Nero—"

He walks out, leaving me alone with my questions. I half-expect to hear a lock turn in the door, but that doesn't happen.

Nero's icy pledge to hunt me down and kill me is enough of a padlock to keep me in place.

I want to get out of this dress, so I head straight for the closet, pulling it open to find it full of clothing in my size. Everything is brand new, and I wonder who bought it all. It has to have been purchased in just the last few hours.

Grabbing a pair of comfy yoga pants and a loose T-shirt, I change my clothes. When I take off the necklace and earrings, I'm tempted to throw them in the trash, just to spite Nero, but I know I've probably pushed my luck enough for now.

Taunting the beast won't get me anywhere.

But what will?

Pacing the room in my bare feet, I think about what he said in his office earlier tonight.

Everyone has a price.

What that really means is that everyone has something they want. Something they're willing to bargain for.

Even Nero.

I have no idea about the inner workings of the Barretti

crime syndicate, but from everything I've seen since getting here, I know that what Nero wants must have to do with this McKenna guy—and he wants it bad. Nero Barretti wouldn't have dressed up in a tuxedo and made the trip uptown if it wasn't important to him.

Important enough to outweigh his thirst for vengeance against me?

There's only one way to find out.

Leaving the bedroom, I venture out into the living area. The apartment is dark, but I can see a light coming from the kitchen area.

Nero's standing by the glow of the open refrigerator, shirtless in a pair of grey sweatpants, drinking a glass of water.

I know looking is a bad idea, but I seem to be full of those tonight, so I let my eyes roam over his toned body, taking in the incredible sight. His chest is broader than I remember, and his abs weren't always so well-defined—or mottled with so many tattoos. He's pure masculine power, and my body shudders, remembering the feel of all that muscle pressed up against me earlier tonight.

But now that he's half-naked... I want to touch the artwork, trace the lines with my fingers.

Or tongue.

"Need something, Princess?" Nero's cutting voice jerks my gaze up to meet his face. He looks smug, like he knows exactly what I'm thinking.

I gulp. "I want to talk to you," I say, holding his eyes. I feel like I'm staring down a predator, trying not to show weakness. "To come to some arrangement. I think we can help each other."

"Can we now?" Nero's gaze turns hotter, full of suggestion. "And how, exactly, do you plan on *helping* me?"

"Not like *that*!" I blurt, even as my taut, aching nipples

inform me that yes, they would be amenable. I take another deep breath. "I know that you want something from McKenna. In order to get it, you need to get close to him. He's not incorruptible, no one is. But you have to find a weakness, a way into his circle. And they will never let a Barretti in."

Nero scowls. "What's your point?"

I place the palms of my hands flat on the kitchen island and lean forward.

"I can help you. I know those people; I grew up in that world. I can get you close to McKenna. Close enough to make whatever deal you need to make."

"And how do you propose doing that?"

Again, Nero's face is icy. Expressionless. I press ahead.

"By posing as your fiancée. I'll work my old social contacts and get us the invites to the right events. Showing up with me on your arm will give you a respectability you could never have alone—at least, enough to get close to McKenna."

Nero's eyes widen, and I take a small pleasure in knowing that I surprised him.

"You want to get engaged?" he asks.

"I want to pretend to be engaged," I correct him. "You'll seem like you're more legit. The kind of guy a family man like McKenna can do business with. You'll get whatever deal you're after, but I want something in return."

Nero snorts. "Of course you do."

"I want protection for me and Teddy." I state clearly, my heart pounding in my chest. He hasn't shut me up, or sent me away just yet, which means this is possible. I have a chance. "I help you score this deal with McKenna, and you give me your word, the two of us will be safe. From you—and everyone in the organization."

"You're not in a position to be making demands, Princess." Nero strolls closer, power coiled, like a panther ready to pounce. "In case you've forgotten, you owe me. A debt that can only be settled in blood."

"My father's betrayal was ten years ago," I point out. "And he's long since dead."

"He wasn't the only one who betrayed us," Nero says cryptically. "A debt's a debt."

Fuck. I try one last time, praying with everything I have that some part of Nero is still thoughtful. The man who assessed the odds before striking.

"Are you really willing to throw away whatever it is you've been working for?" I challenge him. "Because if tonight proved anything, I'm your only hope. You'll never get close to the guy again. You have no idea how that world operates. So tell me this, Nero: Do you want revenge, or do want McKenna?"

My question hangs in the air, and Nero keeps his face stoic, not giving away his thoughts one bit. It feels like an eternity as I wait for him to mull it over—my fear winding tighter in my chest with every moment, until I can hardly breathe.

When Nero's answer comes, it's a low, reluctant growl.

"Deal."

Oh my God.

I give a nod, then flee back to my room, putting as much distance as possible between us before he changes his mind. I turn the lock once I'm inside and collapse onto the bed, my entire body shaking with the force of what I've just achieved.

A way out.

One shot to keep my brother safe—and myself alive to see it.

This isn't going to be easy, but I will make this work, no matter what.

The only things that I'm not sure of is if I can pull this off... Without falling back into Nero Barretti's arms.

7

LILY

THE BED IS HEAVENLY, and I sleep well, despite everything. When I wake up, sunlight streams in through the curtains, and I can tell that it's late in the morning. The apartment is silent, as far as I can tell, but maybe it's so big that it muffles the sound.

Either way, I have no idea what to do now.

By some miracle—and my desperate quick thinking last night—I've managed to broker some kind of temporary peace with Nero. But I already know, I'm on the clock to prove my usefulness and deliver access to Ian McKenna.

Where do I even begin?

By cleaning up, for starters. I reluctantly get out of bed, and head for the bathroom, which immediately puts me in a better mood. After so many years of shitty apartments with mold problems, I forgot that bathrooms could be this nice. It's the little things you take for granted until they're gone. There's not just an epic shower in here, but a jacuzzi tub, too. I promise myself that I'll find a chance to use it at some point—I miss the relaxing, warm bubbles, soothing my aching muscles while I drift off to sleep in a haze of steam. I have to admit to myself that it's nice to be back in these kinds of surroundings. Everything is shiny and new and luxurious.

And if that makes me shallow... Well, I prefer to call it looking on the bright side of my captivity.

Speaking of which... After I shower and get dressed in a preppy, luxurious silk shirtdress, I venture out of the bedroom, wondering what I'll find. A part of me expects to find a guard there, but there's no one around. Technically, I could walk right out the door if I wanted, but I know that Nero was serious last night.

He isn't going to let me go twice.

I feel a shiver, remembering the deadly promise in his gaze. God, it's still hard to reconcile the dangerous man I'm around now with the boy that I was head over heels for. Nero used to bring me roses, sweet little gifts just to make me smile. He even talked about us getting married someday, and while I knew even then that they were the idle daydreams of a boy raised in a different world, I loved the way I felt with him.

Safe. Cherished. Like the most precious prize of all.

Well, I'm safe now—but in a very different way. Trapped, and bound by a blood debt I have only a slim chance of paying.

I shake my head. The only way out of this is by looking forward, not back, so pushing those distracting memories to the back of my mind, I move past the exit door, and into the living area. My stomach growls and I realize I can't remember the last time I ate. They probably served a delicious dinner at the gala last night, and I missed out on it.

I grab some orange juice out of the refrigerator and toast a bagel, taking in my surroundings in the light of day. The main loft is a stunning space, all masculine leather furniture with an industrial, vintage edge, but there's something off about it—it's missing that personal touch. No photos, no mementos... I would guess that it was professionally decorated by someone who didn't know Nero very well.

But that's not a surprise: He's not an easy man to know. And now that he's running the Barretti organization... I would guess any hint of his personal life could prove a weakness. Give his enemies something to hold onto.

I've just finished my breakfast when I hear a thud, coming from somewhere in the loft. It's followed by a manly grunt, and the sounds of grappling.

I slide off the stool and look around. I didn't think anyone was here, but I follow the sound to a staircase, leading down a level. Pushing open the door, I find a massive gym space. There's every kind of exercise equipment I can think of, and in the middle of the room, there's a makeshift fighting ring, where Nero is training with a tall, Nordic-looking guy.

"Keep your weight back," he barks at Nero, circling. "Now, again."

Nero lunges at him, getting him in a complex gripping headlock, and the pair grapple, grunting and panting with the exertion.

I watch, fascinated. The fighting style is complex, and the moves both men make are downright impressive. It's almost like dancing, and I admire the fluidity and grace on display.

And that's not all that's on display. Nero is shirtless once again, and I drink in the sight of him: Those dark tattoos bare and sweaty, his muscles flexing with every move. My blood runs hot, watching as he gets his trainer in a brutal hold, pinning him to the mat until he taps out, gasping.

I shiver. Nero in action is undeniably powerful, taking down the mountain of his trainer with his bare hands like that. I know I should be repulsed by the violence on display, but instead, I find it intoxicating. *Sexy.* I can't tear my gaze away.

Which is when Nero looks up and sees me standing there.

I want to turn and run, but I force myself to walk forwards instead, joining him on the edge of the mat as he gulps from a bottle of water and shakes his trainer's hand.

"Next week?" he asks.

Nero nods. "I'll let you know what time."

The trainer gives me a curious glance, then grabs his stuff and leaves. Nero starts stacking workout equipment, making a point not to talk to me, until I finally roll my eyes and sigh. "If we're going to work together, you can at least acknowledge my existence."

"Was that what you were doing snooping down here?" he asks, "*Existing*."

I control my temper. "What kind of fighting is that? I've never seen it before."

"It's called Krav Maga." He answers abruptly. "It's an Israeli fighting system."

I have to wonder if studying it is how he got so ripped. He has a fighter's body now. There's nothing lean or soft about him. I have to wonder what he'd be like now, on top of me, pinning me roughly down, *thrusting into me...*

"We need to talk," I say, changing the subject for the sake of my own sanity.

"Talking's the last thing you need." Nero flashes me a look full of dark foreboding, and dammit, I get goosepimples at the commanding tone in his voice. He turns and stalks back to the stairs. I hurry after him.

"If I'm going to help, I need to know more about what's going on with McKenna," I say, following him upstairs to the loft. "What do you need from him?"

"That's family business."

I know what that means. It's code for *mind your own business*. These mafia guys are big on discretion.

"I need to be in the loop on this one," I insist. "How else am

I supposed to get you close to the guy, help set up whatever deal you need to make?"

Nero crosses to the kitchen area and starts programming the expensive Italian coffee machine.

"I mean it, Nero," I try again. "I can't do anything if I don't know the game plan. We have to work together on this."

Nero finally turns back to face me. He clenches his jaw for a long moment, searching my face. "I don't trust you."

"Well, that's fine," I reply. "The feeling's mutual. Doesn't change our situation though."

Nero sighs. "Fine," he says. But still, he makes me wait while he pours a cup of coffee and moves to sit at the table. I take a seat, too. "McKenna is on the City Council," he begins. "He's on the Planning Committee, overseeing zoning and development. Hell, he's the chairman of the whole damn thing. Elected because he's so honest and virtuous." Nero's lips twist in grim amusement.

"You have something you want to build?" I ask.

Nero nods. "The past couple of years, I've quietly been buying up buildings downtown around Canal Street. Old warehouses, apartment buildings... I've got the whole city block locked up now. I figured, if the fucking developers could hollow out this city, then why couldn't we get a piece of the action, too? Prime Manhattan real estate, ready to be torn down and redeveloped. I'm talking, luxury condos, retail, office buildings... *If* we get the development approved."

My mind races. "You need McKenna's vote," I say, realizing just how much rides on this deal. "My God, if a project like this went through, that land would be worth a fortune. Hundreds of millions."

"Maybe even billions." Nero agrees, meeting my gaze with a triumphant smile.

Then he seems to remember himself. The smile slips. "This

is it. The big one. I have the construction crews lined up, and the plans are drawn. I want this project underway and breaking ground in the next three months. We thought we could buy McKenna off. Cash in a briefcase, same as the rest of those corrupt fuckers. But he's not playing ball"

"Because he wants more than money," I agree, nodding. "He wants power. So how will you talk him into it, if I get you in the same room as him?"

Nero gives a dangerous smirk. "You leave that to me, Princess. I have my ways."

My blood runs cold. I'm sure he does. But that's not my problem.

All that matters is fulfilling my end of the deal—and keeping my brother safe.

I stand. "I better get to work then. But I need one more thing from you."

Nero arches an eyebrow. "What's that?"

"Your credit card."

WITH NERO'S platinum AmEx nestled safely in my new bag, I direct my driver to Marche Salon. Yes, I have a driver now, one of Nero's heavies outfitted with a Mercedes G-wagon and a scowl. I'm under no illusions, he's a prison guard designed to keep tabs on me, but as I drive through the city in style, I try not to let it get to me.

I'm on a mission now. Get to Ian McKenna.

And my #1 way of doing that?

Get to his wife.

Fiona mentioned getting her hair done at this salon when I overheard her at the gala, so I waltz through the front doors and bat my eyelashes at the girl on reception, begging for an appointment. "My ends are *begging* for a trim," I coo, playing the pampered Park Avenue princess. "I'll take anything. Pretty please?"

She checks the books. "I did just have a last-minute cancellation, I can squeeze you in with Frederik?"

"Angel!" I beam—and slide a twenty across the desk. "I so appreciate it."

I'm whisked back to get a long shampoo and scalp massage, which is so blissful, I almost forget about my top-secret mission here.

Almost.

When I'm settled in the salon chair with my stylist, Frederik, I get my game face back on and make the usual small talk: guy troubles, vacation, charity work, super happy life.

Not a word is true, but I keep it vague.

"You're a lifesaver," I tell him, as he lops a couple of inches off my straw split-ends. "Fiona said that this was the place to come for miracles. Fiona McKenna?" I add.

He brightens. "Oh, isn't she a doll? You just missed her."

"What a shame! She said she practically lives here, with all the political events she and Ian attend."

Frederik nods. "I like to joke that she's my best customer. But tonight's not a political event. They're going to the ballet. Ian surprised her with tickets for her birthday last week. Isn't he the sweetest?"

"He really is," I agree with a smile. And so is Frederik, giving me the insider info I need.

We finish up my hair, and I pay—with a healthy tip. The minute I'm back in the car, I bring up the internet on my phone, and find ballet performances tonight.

Bingo. New York City Ballet are performing a special charity event of Don Quixote, in aid of some kids' refuge. This must be it.

I send Nero a text message.

McKenna will be at the ballet tonight.

I send a link to the performance info, and his response comes less than a minute later. One short word.

Fine.

That's it. No thank you or—God forbid—a little praise for doing a good job.

I should know better than to expect it. Nero is clearly still bound up in the past, and the way my father betrayed his family.

I just hope that things go well tonight. The sooner I secure him this vote, the sooner I can move on with my life.

And never lay eyes on the man again.

8

NERO

"THIS IS A WASTE OF DAMN TIME."

I glance at Chase in the mirror. He's standing behind me, watching as I fuck up tying my bowtie.

"Seriously, the ballet?" he continues. "What happened to doing business the right way? McKenna takes a walk with a couple of our guys, maybe we send a message to his wife. You can bet, he'll be voting whichever fucking way we want. Not stupid trips out in your best tuxedo. C'mon man, this is beneath you." Chase scowls.

I know he's got my back, but he's losing patience with this McKenna thing. I don't love it either, but I've got my eyes on the bigger prize here. The payoff. And I'm determined to do whatever is necessary to get it.

"No," I reply. "What's stupid is threatening a big-shot politician. Do you want the FBI crawling up our asses again? That didn't exactly work out well last time, did it?"

Chase's frown deepens. The last time the FBI came after the Barretti organization, my father wound up in prison—

where he's still sitting to this day. It took us years to rebuild, and I'm in no hurry to mess with the feds again.

"Still, I don't like this plan," he grumbles. "That bitch shouldn't be walking around like a free woman. We can't trust her."

"You think I don't know that?" I challenge him, old betrayals still slicing through my gut. "She's part of the reason my father's been gone half my life. I wouldn't trust her an inch. But we can *use* her."

Chase smirks. "Oh yeah? And how are you liking *using her* so far? Did she pick up any tricks in Vegas?"

My jaw clenches, and I have to control my temper. Even thinking about the other men who may have laid a hand on Lily in the past ten years makes my blood hot with fury. Hell, I broke every bone in that street punk's hand just for daring to touch her.

There's no saying what I would do to any man who'd tried more.

But I don't need Chase knowing just how crazy that woman still makes me. I'm supposed to be untouchable. The boss.

I force myself to let out a casual laugh. "None of your damn business," I say, with a big wink. "But let's just say... I have no complaints."

Chase laughs, relaxing. Lucky bastard. I've been wound tight since the moment I laid eyes on Lily Fordham, the kind of aching tension there's only one way to relieve. And dammit, I've tried: My cock's nearly raw with the way I've been jacking off, night and day. Just the scent of her is enough to make me ravenous; the way she runs her tongue over her lips when she's nervous.

When she wants me.

I wanted to put her in her place, show her who's in charge

now, but fuck, it's hell being in the same apartment as her, knowing she's just down the hall. I've nearly thrown her down and sated my hunger with her slick cunt a hundred times. Given it to her rough and deep, until she's screaming my name; show her what she walked away from.

Just who she betrayed.

I give up on the bowtie and throw it down instead. *Fuck.* It's that betrayal I've got to hold onto. Chase is right: I can't trust her. She already blew this organization wide apart ten years ago, conspiring with her father to sell me out, blinding me with her innocent act, while she was taking me for a fool.

I won't be her fool again.

I hear the click of heels on the floor, and then Lily arrives in the living room. I turn to look at her, and damn, if she isn't still the most beautiful thing I've ever laid eyes on. A princess draped in rosy pink satin, clinging to every luscious curve.

The kind of body men go to wars over. The kind of face that makes them believe in God.

Fuck. Yet again, I find myself wondering why I didn't have Chase just leave her body in a shallow grave in Vegas, along with the fucker who was trying it on. Debt paid. Score settled. End of the matter.

But I knew, deep down, the moment I laid eyes on her again, I could never let her come to harm. At my hand, or anyone else's.

I just hope she holds up her side of this twisted bargain and then gets the fuck out of my life again.

"Where's your necklace?" I ask as my eyes lock on her long, bare throat.

"I can't wear the same thing to a social function two nights in a row," she says, with a faint sneer.

"Or maybe you're thinking you can get away this time without the tracker?" I retort.

"I'm not doing that again," she says. She has the nerve to sound almost insulted.

"You expect me to take you at your word?" I growl.

"I don't expect anything from you."

Her withering look adds an undertone of anger to the desire I feel, and I want to put my fist through a wall. This alliance isn't going to work if I can't get myself together.

But when she looks at me like that... It brings out the beast in me. Like she's superior. Untouchable.

And we both know that's bullshit. I've touched her. I know her moans of pleasure and the taste of her sweet honey. She can't take that away, no matter how much she might despise me now.

I grab my jacket, and nod to the door. "Don't forget what I said, Princess. If you run again—"

"I won't." she cuts me off. "We have an agreement."

I snort. "And you're a woman of honor, huh? Don't play those games with me. You're forgetting. I know all your lies."

I walk out, knowing she'll follow. She's smart enough to know she's on thin ice with me, at least. The car's waiting downstairs, and I get in, trying to ignore her as she settles in the backseat beside me, fussing with her hair and arranging her skirts.

The skirts I'm hungry to shove up around her waist. The gold silk hair I want knotted around my fist as I ride her, hard, until she breaks.

I clench my fists and look out of the window, aware of every damn shift of her lithe body.

How could I forget, when she's around, there's nothing else in the world.

I hate that she holds my attention so thoroughly. She doesn't even have to try. It's just like when we were younger. I lusted after her for years when we were growing up, fixated to

the point of obsession. I'd volunteer to run important documents out to her father on Long Island, just to catch a glimpse
of her in that jailbait Catholic girl uniform, hanging out in the
kitchen after school. Not that I could do more than look. She
was off-limits, out of my league. Hell, she was too young, as
innocent as they come up in her ivory tower, pampered and
protected from the likes of me.

Until she wasn't.

Until I'd catch her watching me with heat in her eyes, a
flush in those pretty cheeks.

Until the day she turned sixteen, and I had no excuses left
why I couldn't steal a taste of heaven for myself.

"I don't want a repeat of the gala this time."

Her voice snaps me back to the present as we arrive at the
theater. Lily gives me a cool, disdainful look. "You need to
make an effort. And if you can't? Then just keep quiet and let
me do the talking."

"Fine with me," I snap back. The superiority in her eyes
should ease my hard-on, but fuck if it doesn't make me want her
more. "It's about time you earned your keep."

She flushes, angry. "I'm the one who even found out about
tonight," she replies.

"What do you want, a medal?"

I get out of the car and march up the front steps, making
her hurry to keep up. That's how I need to keep this—never let
her forget even for a moment who's boss. It's her life in my
hands, and she needs to remember that.

But of course, Lily always demanded the upper hand.
"Would it kill you to smile?" she murmurs, as we step into the
crowded lobby.

"Not everyone can just slip on a mask and be a different
person," I reply. "But you were always good at lying, weren't
you?"

I see a flash of hurt on her face, but it's quickly smoothed by that perfect smile again. "You should be grateful. My lies are going to get you what you want."

What I want is this woman on her knees with her lips wrapped around my cock. Begging for another inch. Swallowing every last drop.

"Careful, Princess," I growl, stepping closer. Her eyes widen, and she inhales fast. Fearful.

Good.

"You're the one who should be grateful, that I'm allowing your heart to keep beating another night. Or maybe I should call my guys, and have them pay your brother a visit..."

"No!" Lily blurts. "Please. I... I'm sorry," she manages, even with hatred flashing in her eyes. "I'll behave."

Damn. What I wouldn't give to see her *behave* herself in a dark, empty room. Or maybe I wouldn't even wait for that. Fuck, we could put on a show right here that these rich assholes would never forget: Her dress yanked down to her waist, her screams of pleasure echoing for everyone to hear—

Get a fucking grip.

I block the vision, and stride away, into the building. The lobby of the theater is big and packed with people. They haven't opened the doors to the auditorium yet, so everyone is milling about in this space.

I look around. There's expensive art on the walls and marble beneath our feet. I have plenty of money, and I can afford nice things. But I can never understand this decadence. It's so over the top. I always feel out of place in an event like this, like everyone can see my money comes soaked in blood.

Lily's a different story. She slips right into character, proving my point about how good she is at lying. She's a lady who lunches, walking around and greeting people that she hasn't seen in ten years as if they're close friends. Lies about where she's been are told so convincingly that even I almost believe them.

I despise her in this moment. I'm also impressed.

I tag along in her wake, trying to keep my eyes on the prize, even though I don't see McKenna anywhere yet, but I do see someone else. A man who doesn't quite fit into this crowd, loitering in the back in a cheap suit and tie.

He's watching me.

I turn away. Feds, maybe, or a man from a rival organization. I'm used to the attention, and normally, I wouldn't think twice, but I can feel his gaze on Lily, too, and somehow that makes me want to go throttle him with his cheap tie.

She's off-limits.

"Time to take our seats," Lily says brightly, finishing up chatting to some older couple about the opera. "So lovely to catch up. Babe?" she prompts me, fluttering her eyeslashes.

"Sure thing, Princess."

I fake a smile, and follow her into the luxurious hallway, leading to the auditorium. I don't give a shit about ballet, but at least it will be a break from all this fake social bullshit.

"Well, what have we here?"

A smug English accent announces a new arrival. It's Sebastian Wolfe, a corporate raider, looking like he belongs here with an expensive brunette on his arm.

"Nero Barretti, at the ballet? Now I really have seen everything," he smirks.

I meet his gaze, steely. "Wolfe," I say shortly. "You're still in town? I'm surprised. Considering."

"Considering what?" the brunette asks, clueless.

"Wolfe here lost out on a big acquisition." I say. "Sterling jewelry company. Dropped out of the deal. But that wasn't the only condition, was it?"

I meet his gaze, and Seb's smile falters. I was the one who made him quit the takeover.

Me, and my Colt .85.

"I'm leaving for London tomorrow," he says, hatred burning in his eyes. Men like him hate to lose.

But men like me don't give a fuck.

"Good." I reply. "You won't be missed." I take Lily's arm and keep walking.

"What was that?" she hisses in my ear as soon as we're out of earshot.

"Nothing. Just a business acquaintance."

"Right. Friendly."

I give her a glare. "What do you expect, Princess? I'm not a Bible salesman. You know what I do in my line of work."

She recoils, and I'm both relieved and stung. Yeah, she might like to think she's so much better than me, but we're both part of the same rotten empire now.

We find our seats with the help of an usher and get settled. I'm growing impatient, knowing that the show is about to start, and we haven't even seen McKenna yet. He's the whole reason we came.

"Can you sit still?" Lily whispers, her satin dress touching my thigh. She's pressed close, and her scent is so damn distracting, I want to bolt.

"Ashamed to be seen in public with me?" I ask, already knowing the answer. Luckily, I'm saved from her reply by a couple squeezing into the seats next to us.

"Nero!" The woman's face lights up in surprise, but she's not sneering like everyone else in the building.

She leans in to kiss my cheek, and I notice Lily tense beside me. Jealousy?

"Juliet," I greet her, before giving a nod to her husband as he follows.

Caleb Sterling.

My half-brother.

Technically, at least. I don't think of him as family. After all, we only recently discovered we shared a father, thanks to a long-ago affair. Throw in the fact I was blackmailing him, and you don't exactly have a recipe for a happy family reunion.

"What a nice coincidence," Juliet says warmly, as they take their seats. "I've been wondering how you are."

"Can't complain," I reply. Juliet's the one who brokered peace between us, and I have a lot of respect for her loyalty and guts. "How was the honeymoon?"

"It was amazing." She reaches over and takes Caleb's hand, giving it a happy squeeze. "We were on a private island, nobody around. Bliss. She shoots a curious look at Lily, and I make a curt introduction.

"So what brings you to the ballet?" Juliet asks.

"Business."

Juliet grins. "I should have guessed."

"I'm looking to get a moment with an old friend of mine," I continue, scanning the auditorium. "Ian McKenna. Have you seen him yet?"

Caleb looks amused. "You just missed him. He and his wife were called away, something important."

Fuck.

The lights go down before I can reply, and the audience begins to hush. Lily shifts beside me, her arm pressing against mine. Close enough to touch. Her scent lingers, intoxicating, and in the darkness, I can see the rise and fall of her chest in that gown, molded to her breasts.

It's goddamn torture. Trussed up in this tuxedo, way out of my comfort zone. Stuck sitting beside the woman who torments me every time she draws breath.

This whole evening was a mistake.

I bolt to my feet.

"Where are you going?" Lily asks, tugging on my sleeve.

"Fuck this bullshit." I shake her free. "I'm going to get a drink."

I walk out as the music begins and I don't look back.

Because even glancing at Lily right now is a temptation I don't want to face. I swore I wouldn't be her fool again, but dammit if I don't want to drag her straight out of this fancy world...

And back into my bed.

9

LILY

IT'S BEEN three days since the night of the ballet, and I've hit a wall when it comes to Ian McKenna. I've done my research, looking into his staff, background, and other connections for opportunities, but so far, I've found nothing useful. Getting close to him isn't going to be as easy as I hoped.

Meanwhile, I'm still a prisoner. Tied to Nero, whether I like it or not.

I spend most of my time days cooped up in this apartment. Nero is gone when I wake in the morning, and returns so late every night, I sometimes wonder if he even comes back at all.

I wish I didn't care where he laid his head at night. Or with who.

I need to get out of here before I lose my mind, so on a whim, I call my old schoolfriend, Marissa, the one I bumped into at the gala.

"Lily!" she answers with an excited squeal. "I was literally just thinking about you. I was so good to see you again. What's happening?"

"How about lunch?" I suggest.

"Love it. Giselle's at noon?"

"See you there."

I hang up, pleased. At least now I have a reason to get out, and someone to talk to, not just the doubts and insecurities circling in my mind.

I take time picking an outfit. I've already given Nero's credit card a workout, ordering clothes to be delivered to the apartment. Perversely, I've been ordering way OTT designer things, wondering if Nero would confront me. But I guess that would mean acknowledging my existence, which he hasn't done in days.

Not since the ballet.

I knew I was pushing it, goading him the way I did. But since he already thinks I'm a pampered princess, I couldn't help rubbing it in.

Anything to ignore the feelings he inspired in me, that tuxedo barely containing his muscles, looking like a dark, avenging demon striding through the fancy crowds.

I shiver at the memory. Every time he looked at me with hatred in his eyes, it only turned me on more, until it was a relief when he bolted. I don't think I could have endured a couple of hours sitting there beside him, imagining those rough hands on my body, taking their revenge.

That cruel mouth making me moan.

WHEN I ARRIVE AT LUNCH, Marissa is already there waiting for me. It's a rooftop restaurant with panoramic views of the city and a vegan menu. Marissa is flawless with her freshly styled hair and light makeup.

We do the air-kissing thing again, and it's getting easier to take on this role of upper-class socialite. The more I do it, the more it feels like I never left.

But that's a fantasy.

I know I'm not the same person I was before I left. That fact is highlighted by my conversation with Marissa. We both order a salad, but she's so busy telling me all about her exciting life that she barely eats.

"And then we were all in Amalfi for the summer," she says, glowing at the memories—and with the thousand-dollar facial she just recommended. "Oh Lils, you should have been there! The architecture... The art... It was incredible. But what am I saying? You must have been!"

"Mhmm!" I give a vague nod, sipping my iced tea, and wracking my brain for a way to deflect from what I've been doing for the past ten years.

Somehow, I don't think, 'working in a cheap strip club and running for my life' will impress her quite so much. "But never mind travel, I want to hear all about your husband. Tell me everything!"

Marissa beams wider. "We met in Napa, his family has a vineyard there. It was like a fairytale, he swept me off my feet."

As she tells me about their whirlwind romance, the lavish wedding, setting up house together, I try not to feel a pang of envy. After all, this is the life I would be living too.

If the Barretti family hadn't stolen it from me.

In another world, I would be the one gossiping about travel and romance. I dreamed of attending art school in Paris, having a career, and a loving husband, and, yes, a vacation house in the Hamptons, too.

Instead, all I have is a string of fake names and shitty motel leases in my past, and Nero's word he won't kill me when this deal is up.

"I'm glad we're doing this," Marissa says, giving me a genuine smile. "It's nice to catch up with an old friend. Now that you're back in the city, we have to hang out more. Me and Ryan, and you and your fiancé."

Right. Nero is supposed to be my fiancé.

"What are your plans for the afternoon?" she adds, digging into her food.

"Nothing much," I try to sound breezy. "A little shopping, you know."

"Me too!" she exclaims. "I have to find Ryan some hunting gear, but it's not exactly in my wheelhouse." She wrinkles her lip.

"Hunting?" I ask politely.

She nods. "We've been invited to this exclusive retreat at a lodge upstate. Of course, he's never laid a finger on a rifle in his life, so I'm under orders to make him look the part, at the very least, so he doesn't embarrass himself in front of all the VIPs." She gives an affectionate laugh. "It's some male bonding routine, you know how they are. Meanwhile, I'll be enjoying the spa facilities with Fiona and the other wives."

I sit up straighter. "Fiona?" I try to keep my voice casual.

"McKenna," Marissa replies, "You met her the other night."

"That's right. She seems nice. So... She and her husband will be at this retreat, too?" I ask, my heart beating faster.

"Yup. Plus a handful of other business types. You know how it is."

"Sure," I nod along, secretly filing away the info.

Marissa pauses. "But what am I saying? I've been talking about myself this whole time. Tell about you. You mentioned travelling and charity work at the gala, but I want to know more about that hunk I spotted you with."

"Nero?" I gulp, plastering on a smile. "What is there to say? He's... A force of nature."

"I'll say." Marissa gives me a knowing smile. "My god, no

wonder you're walking around with a smile on your face, going home every night to a man like that!"

I pretend to laugh along. She has no idea who Nero is. What he's capable of. But there's something about this charade that makes me feel raw inside. An emotion rises up inside of me that I wasn't expecting when I suggested pretending to be engaged. Regret. And longing, too. Despite everything.

"But you're not wearing a ring," Marissa adds, nodding to my bare hand.

"Oh, right," I wave it dismissively. "My fiancé is a sweetheart, but he doesn't always think about the details. The ring was a touch too big, so I'm having it resized."

"But is it gorgeous?"

"Of course." I lie. "He wouldn't settle for anything but the best."

"I love it!" Marissa claps her hands together. "Look at us now, it's just like we always pictured when we were younger. Two men madly in love with us."

She toasts my glass, and I follow suit. The irony is, she's right. I always did dream about getting married to Nero one day. But then again, I had no idea what the real world was like. Looking back now, I was so naïve, even though I didn't realize it at the time. I was in love with him, and it was all that mattered in the world to me. Even when my parents dragged me off one night into witness protection, he was all I cared about. Sure, losing the house and money was hard, but being unable to contact the boy I loved... It felt like just about the worst thing to ever happen to me.

It didn't take me long to find out just how wrong I was about that. There was far worse to come, courtesy of the Barrettis.

. . .

WE FINISH LUNCH, and part with hugs and promises to get together for drinks next week. I'm eager to get back and share my intel with Nero. I tell myself that I just want to move this whole plan along and win my freedom, but deep inside, I know that I have a pointless desire to try to earn his approval.

Talk about a lost cause.

Back at the apartment, the place looks empty, but there's music playing in his office, and when I go looking, I hear the sound of a shower running down the hall.

His bedroom door is open. I can't help peeking in.

The room is large and sparsely decorated, but with a familiar painting hanging above the massive bed.

It can't be...

I step forwards, captivated. A Rothko? I inhale, stunned to see one in real life like this. He's my favorite artist, but I've only ever seen him hanging in galleries and museums. It's huge, one of his red series, the color so vivid it's punching off the canvas. A painting like this must have cost millions...

And Nero has it hanging above his bed?

As I stand there, speechless, I hear a low groan nearby. It's coming from the open bathroom door, which is wafting steam and the sound of running water into the room.

Before I can think it through, I find myself drawn, as if by magnets, over to the doorway.

Nero is naked inside.

I freeze. He's standing with his back to me under the shower jet spray, water running in rivulets over his bare shoulders. The open plan shower means, surprise, I have a perfect view of his ripped, muscular body.

Every inch.

My blood runs hotter. My pulse kicks. I know I should leave but I can't for the life of me move a muscle.

His body is incredible. Sculpted from marble. His shoulders are huge, the muscles along them flexing as he reaches up to run his hand through his hair. My gaze travels down, along the ridges and contours of his toned back and ass. His legs are long and muscular.

I can see the ridges of definition in his back. And that ass...

He lets out another groan, slamming one hand against the wall. And that's when I realize, he has the other hand wrapped around his cock. His grip looks tight as he works it from base to tip, over and over again. He's jerking off furiously under the spray, making low guttural noises with every motion.

I can't look away.

Blood rushes to my cheeks—and then lower. My thighs clench, heat spiraling to my core. His movements are so brash, so undeniably sexual. It's raw, animalistic.

And I can't get enough.

Desire aches inside me, a need that rivals the one I have for oxygen. It's powerful and all-consuming.

And it only gets worse as his pace builds, his groans growing more guttural as he builds to his climax. Muscles bunch up and loosen again all over his body, and I can't help thinking about him thrusting into me, right here in the shower. Using those same muscles to take me. *Claim me.* Groan that desperate tune in my ear.

What would it feel like, to have that ferocious sexuality trained on me, full force?

My legs are weak, watching as his movements grow jerky and labored. I find myself panting in time with him, desire rising, coursing in my veins until—

He turns.

Oh my God!

Our eyes lock as he climaxes with a groan, still pumping his cock as ribbons of come spurt into the shower spray.

Still, he doesn't look away.

I'm shaken to my core. Wound tight. Aching for my own release, and fuck, it's the most erotic moment of my life...

But that passes when his face morphs into an expression of cold amusement. He turns off the shower and grabs a towel from the rack. But he doesn't attempt to cover himself with it. Instead, he rubs his over his head, drying his hair. He wants me to look at his naked body.

And damn, if I do.

"You like what you see, Princess?" He's still hard, amazingly, and I swallow around a lump in my throat because the answer is yes, even though I'd never tell him that. "I had no idea you were such a dirty little voyeur."

I feel shame burn through me at his words but fight to keep my face neutral. I can't let him see that his words have such a strong effect on me.

"You wish," I reply breezily, even though I'm wet. "I came to update you on what I've learned about McKenna. There's a hunting party this weekend, some secluded lodge. A dozen guys and their wives. It could be the perfect opportunity to get close to him. A captive audience. And I know how you like those."

I'm amazed I can keep my voice steady, after what just happened. I feel like I got hit by a truck—the force of Nero's sexual power.

"That's all?" Nero asks, with a dangerous smile. "Or do you need to come clean up?" he gestures to the shower, and I scowl.

"Never in a million years."

I turn on my heel and leave, racing back to my own room. I slam the door behind me and sink against it, taking a moment to catch my breath.

What just happened?

I whimper in regret. I shouldn't have allowed myself to watch him like that but God, he's sexy. Too sexy. He pushes all my buttons, and the sight of his fist working up and down his thick shaft is going to stay with me, fueling dirty fantasies for years.

The door suddenly opens, sending me stumbling away. Nero walks in, fully clothed this time.

"Ever heard of knocking?!" I protest, still unsteady—and not just because of the surprise.

"I'll do what I want in my own damn house," Nero drawls. His gaze burns over me, like he can see my body is still turned on. "What I want... Or *who.*"

My flush deepens. "Whom," I correct him icily.

He scowls. "I came to tell you, your tip paid off," he says. "I pulled some strings and got an invite to this hunting party."

Relief washes over me. A little distance from Nero is just what I need. Maybe a weekend alone will give me a chance to forget about this hunger I have for him.

"Good," I reply, clipped. "I hope it works out for you."

I turn away, and he gives a low chuckle. "You'll do more than hope, Princess. You'll make sure of it. We leave tomorrow afternoon."

What?

"We?" I repeat nervously.

Nero smiles. Deadlier than any scowl. "You think I'm letting you out of my sight for a whole weekend? Besides, how would it look if I showed up without my loving fiancé?"

He reaches out to touch my cheek, and I flinch away. His smile only widens. "That's right, you like to look, not touch. Well, who knows, Princess? Maybe you'll find something else to watch while we're there."

He walks out before I can throw a vase at him.

10

LILY

I'VE BEEN SHOPPING at Target and the clearance section at Marshall's for the past ten years, but some things stick with you. I have no problem swiping Nero's credit card shamelessly, again and again, as I go from store to store.

After all, I have an assignment now.

I started off my day buying hunting gear, practically throwing money at the guy in the men's department at Bergdorf's to put together the outfits Nero will need for this trip of his. Now, I'm on a mission to revamp my own wardrobe, upstairs in the luxurious surroundings of the designer ateliers, the kind of place that gives out flutes of champagne in a velvet-draped room while saleswomen parade things in front of me.

Even though I'm furious at Nero for dragging me along with him this weekend, I admit to myself that it's pretty wonderful to be back in the lap of luxury, with people catering to my every whim. For so long, *I* was the one working my ass off, running around for tip money. Now, I'm the one lounging on a comfortable couch, saying 'yes' and 'no' with a brief nod of my head as everyone flocks to bring me gorgeous outfits.

"I think I have just the thing for you," a young saleswoman says with an excited smile on her face. She has a gorgeous blue dress draped over her arm, and I finish off my champagne as I stand. "It comes in a white, too, but this is perfect with your coloring."

"June, you are amazing," I say as she hands it over. I hold out the dress and try not to think about whether or not Nero would like it.

I don't care if he does.

At least, that what I tell myself.

"Do you want to try it on?" she asks eagerly. "I can add it to the room."

The room that is already overflowing. I smile. "Yes, please." Ensuring Nero gets a massive balance on his credit card is just my way of taking a small bit of revenge against him for messing with my emotions. Not that I'll let him know that.

No, as far as he's concerned, I couldn't care less about his sexual games. The stunt he pulled in the shower... I'm officially blocking it from my mind.

And as for my heart? I need to keep that thing locked up tight, even if I am struggling with past feelings surging to the surface. *Especially* because of that. I shouldn't feel anything for him other than disdain with the way he's been acting, but somehow, my body hasn't gotten the memo.

My heart, my body... he has a way of affecting every part of me, even as my mind screams at the rest of me to see sense and resist.

I follow June into the dressing room and take the dress from her before she leaves. Sliding the silk over my head, I smile as I see the way the fabric falls. It sure beats the cheap fabrics I've been wearing at the strip club, cheap garments I don't mind getting covered with beer and rancid cologne.

I reach back and try to zip it up, but I can't quite reach.

Going to the door, I crack it open and peek my head out. The area just outside of the dressing room has couches and a pedestal in front of three full-length mirrors.

"June?" I call out. "Can you help me with the zipper?"

"I can help you."

I jolt at the sight of a woman sitting on one of the couches, wearing a basic navy pantsuit. I didn't notice her before, scrolling on her phone. She's already getting to her feet, so I smile. "Oh, thanks."

I turn my back and let her zip up the dress. "What do you think?" I ask, assessing my reflection in the mirror. It's a perfect fit. Gorgeous.

"You look very pretty," she says, with a smile.

"Anyone would look good in a dress this expensive," I reply with a laugh. "It's part of the price tag. Are you shopping for anything?" I ask, still examining my reflection. It would be a knockout for dinner, or another party.

Or making Nero regret he ever taunted me.

"That depends," the woman replies. "On you, Lily."

I freeze. "How do you know my name?" I demand, whirling around. But I know the answer before she says anything, I should have guessed it from her boxy suit, and the no-nonsense look in her eyes.

"I'm with the FBI."

My blood runs cold, but I force myself to stay calm—at least, on the outside.

I step off the pedestal and fluff my hair. "What could you possibly want with me?" I ask, playing dumb.

I can tell she doesn't buy it for a second.

"We need to talk to you," she says, handing me a business card.

I refuse to take it. "I have nothing to say to you."

"Oh, I think you do, Lily." She smirks. "At least, if you want your brother to stay safe."

Teddy?

My pulse kicks with panic as she continues: "Go to the Met museum, the Impressionist wing, Degas' *The Dancing Class.* Be there at four."

"No," I protest. "Tell me what's going on right now. I'm not playing your games."

"The Met," she repeats. Then she presses the card into my hand, and walks out, leaving me alone in the dressing room with a five-thousand-dollar dress and a racing heart.

And the knowledge that even though I've been in danger from Nero, the situation has just gotten a whole lot more complicated.

I FINISH PAYING for my shopping spree and watch as employees carry my bags down to where Nero's driver is waiting at the curb.

"Home?" he asks me, looking bored.

"It's Nero's home, not mine." I can't help saying. "But I'd like to stop at the Met first. There's a new exhibition," I babble, trying not to seem suspicious, but the guy is already pulling away, not caring.

Traffic is heavy, and I nibble on my bottom lip as I keep checking the time. The presence of the FBI is bad news all around. What do they want with me? They must have been watching Nero to even know I'm here, but Nero will lose his mind if he finds out that I'm meeting them for a hush-hush discussion.

Rule number one of the mafia: Talking to the Feds gets you killed.

Or worse.

We finally pull up outside the museum. "Are you coming in?" I blurt, nervous. "The Monet exhibit is amazing."

The driver, Kyle, stares back at me. "I'll wait."

"OK!"

I hurry inside, grabbing a map and info brochure, and playing tourist in case the driver—or any one of Nero's other guys—did follow me, after all. I act causal, gazing at the art and following the female agent's directions until I find the meeting spot. I only see other visitors around, so I take a seat on the bench in front of the painting and wait.

I'm not waiting long.

"Lily. You're looking well."

I turn as an older man casually takes position on the bench beside me. He's in his fifties, wearing a button-down and chinos, with tortoiseshell spectacles on his face.

I haven't seen him in ten years.

"Agent Greggs," I say, my unease growing.

He looks surprised. "You remember me?"

I clench my jaw. "I remember everything about that night."

Sneaking home from a tryst with Nero only to find my parents waiting with their bags packed, and this strange man telling me that we had to leave immediately, in the dead of night.

Telling me that my life as Lily Fordham was over.

I swallow hard. "I thought you'd be retired by now," I say, unable to keep the bitterness from my voice. "A cushy golden watch, courtesy of putting Roman Barretti behind bars. Didn't they give you a medal for making my dad give testimony against him?"

He nods, and I snort. "Well, good for you. Never mind that I lost everything. You might have become a big shot at the FBI for locking up a big-time Mob boss, but you're not the hero in my story."

Agent Greggs exhales. "I'm sorry, Lily. And I'm sorry about your dad. I heard he passed. But you should know, he did what he did to protect you. You, and your brother."

I fold my arms, hating the old feelings of betrayal and grief whirling in my chest.

"He wanted you to have a safe life, away from the Barrettis," Agent Greggs continues. "So, imagine my surprise when I heard you were back in town. On Nero's arm, no less. His apparent fiancée."

Fuck. They have been watching closely.

I stare straight ahead, refusing to show my emotions. "Why am I here?" I ask. "Don't get me wrong, I love the Impressionists, but the company isn't ideal."

Agent Greggs sighs. "I'm here to help you, Lily. I know you would never come back to New York or be seen with him without a hell of a good reason."

"Maybe I just missed the pizza here." I say flippantly, masking my clammy hands and pounding heart. I have one eye on the door, terrified that Kyle will walk in and see us together.

Terrified Nero will find out and exact a merciless price for my betrayal.

Agent Greggs reads my mind. "Look, whatever Nero has roped you into, whatever threat's he's making, we can keep you and Teddy safe."

"I don't need help," I lie stubbornly. I don't trust Nero...

... But I can't trust the FBI, either.

A group of foreign tourists enters the room, chattering loudly. Agent Greggs leans closer, dropping his voice. "Nero's a dangerous man, Lily. You know that. The FBI's been working on the Barretti organization for a long time. We're going to take him down, and you can be a part of that. Don't you want revenge for everything they put your family through?"

I pause. Yes, I do. Desperately. But not if it means putting

Teddy at risk. Right now, Nero's given me his word that Teddy is under his protection off at college and no harm will come to him.

The Feds can't give me the same guarantee.

"I'm not sure what you think I can do for you," I say vaguely. "I don't know anything about the Barretti business."

Agent Greggs narrows his eyes. "I don't believe that for a minute. You're a smart woman, Lily, and right now, you're closer to Nero than anyone. Under the same roof."

"So, what, you want me to spy on him?" I retort.

"Perhaps," he nods. "Help us build the case against him, and destroy the Barretti organization, once and for all."

I see someone who looks like Kyle walk in and freeze in terror—before realizing, it's just another hulking guy. But it's a warning—I've stayed long enough.

I get to my feet. "Why should I believe anything you tell me?" I ask Agent Greggs in a low voice. Even if the Feds and I share a goal—getting free from Nero Barretti—I don't know if I'm better off without them. "You swore to my father that his testimony would bring down the whole syndicate, but here we are, ten years later, and all it ever did was tear our family apart."

He grabs my arm to stop me from leaving.

"Think about it," he says urgently. "Cooperate. Because we can be your friend... Or we can be your enemy. It's your choice."

I shiver at the threat and wrench my arm away.

"Don't hold your breath."

I EXIT THE MUSEUM, and climb in the back of the waiting car, shaken by the encounter—and just how complicated my life is getting.

First Nero wants me dead, now the FBI are circling too,

trying to turn me into an informant to help with all their plans. It feels like I'm walking on a tightrope over a shark-infested pool. One wrong move, and I'll go tumbling down.

But if I can keep my balance...

I take a deep breath. As tempting as it is to have some backup, go running to the Feds and let them take care of everything, I'm not that naïve anymore. My goal is still the same as the moment I laid eyes on Nero in Vegas: Keep my brother safe, and stay alive myself.

Whoever gives me the best chance of that will be my temporary ally, no matter what.

"Nero says to pack, he'll meet you at his office," Kyle says, when we pull up at Nero's place.

I nod, glad I have a little more time to pull myself together before facing him. "I won't be long."

I head upstairs to the apartment, Kyle following with the bags. I head straight for my bedroom and close the door, pulling out the card the female agent gave me.

Agent DiMedio.

555-637-8290

I can't keep it. For all I know, Nero is having every square inch of my space searched the minute I leave. And if he found it...

I commit the phone number to memory, then find the pack of matches I have in the bathroom to light candles and burn the tiny scrap in the sink until there's nothing but ash.

I rinse it down the drain, breathing easier once all trace of the meeting is gone.

I know, the Feds won't quit so easily, but for now, I have bigger things to worry about.

Like this weekend away with Nero.

I turn my attention to packing and make quick work of the task. We'll only be gone the weekend but running in these circles requires being ready for anything. That means lots of clothing and accessories—for the both of us. For daytime, I've assembled all kinds of casually glamorous outfits to fit in with the other wives and girlfriends, but when it comes to nightwear, it's all bulky flannel, as loose and unflattering as they come.

Just in case Nero get any ideas.

Or I do.

I TRY to get my game face on during the ride to Nero's office. I've only had to be around the man for a few hours at a time, so the prospect of a whole weekend playing loved-up fiancée is making my stomach tangle up in knots.

Just how far will our act have to go?

Holding hands? Touching? Kissing?

I flash back to him in the shower, and feel my whole body tighten with the memory. His body under the water, the low animal groans he made, the sheer power of his masculine sex appeal...

I can't help it, the attraction that burns whenever he's nearby. And if that power was unleashed, *on me...*

The car comes to a stop. "Inside," Kyle orders, so I climb out and follow him down an alley and into a back entrance of a building. I can tell from the noise and smells that it's the same building I was brought to when I was bound and blindfolded. This time, I'm able to look around.

Just as I suspected then, we're at the club on 14th street. The Barrettis used it as a meeting spot and general hangout when I was younger. The place has had a revamp since I saw it last, with chic leather booths and dark corners draped in brocade curtains. I clock Avery, the brunette woman, behind the bar, and a few guys drinking, before heading through another door and into the bowels of the club.

Here, the walls are concrete, and doors are locked tight, hiding what sins, I don't even want to know. But as I follow Kyle deeper into the maze of hallways, I hear noise up ahead.

What sounds like muffled cries of pain, and a man begging.

"Please... Stop. I can't..."

A door flings open, just as we pass, revealing a terrible sight in the room: A half-naked man dangling, bruised and bloody, his wrists bound to a pipe above his head.

His face is cut and bleeding, features mangled, with terrible cuts and bruises all over his naked chest.

I gasp, my hand flying to my mouth in shock at the horrific scene.

He lifts his head at the sound. "Is someone there?" he slurs, pitifully. "Please..."

And then Nero steps into view. His knuckles bloody. Splatters on his shirt.

And a cold, merciless look in his eyes.

He balls his fist and strikes the man in the face with a dull crack, then follows with a brutal set of jabs to his ribs and stomach.

The man howls in pain.

"I'm sorry." He sobs. "Please..."

"Sorry isn't good enough," Nero replies calmly, hitting him again, but the man keeps begging, even when the sound is garbled by the blood in his mouth.

I think I'm going to be sick. I stumble back, my footsteps echoing.

Nero pauses his torture. He sees me there through the open door, but there's no reaction on his face. He just calmly turns to the other men.

"Finish the job."

Nero steps into the hallway, heading to an office nearby.

He doesn't say anything. Doesn't even acknowledge what I just saw.

I follow in a daze. I want to run for the hills, but what am I supposed to do? I'm in his territory. Every exit barred.

Besides, there's no place I can hide from what I just witnessed.

Nero enters the office and goes to the ensuite bathroom area. He calmly washes the blood off his hands and strips the stained shirt over his head.

"Ready to go?" he asks, grabbing a fresh shirt from a hook on the wall.

"Go?" I echo, still unsure if I'm going to be sick. The blood... The screams of pain...

Nero looks at me blankly. "The trip upstate?" he reminds me. "It was your big idea."

And then it sinks in. I'm going away for a secluded weekend in the woods.

With a complete monster.

11

LILY

I'M HAVING a hard time pulling myself together as I sit in the back of the car with Nero. My side is pressed into the door, trying to keep my distance without being too obvious about it.

I knew that Nero must have done terrible things to be the man he is today, sitting on top of the Barretti crime empire. Hell, he's threatened my life more than once since I got here. But knowing it and seeing it up close, blood and all, is different. I don't know what to do.

We're driven to the docks, where a helicopter is waiting. I've never been in one before, but that's the least of my concerns right now. I climb aboard in a daze and take my seat behind the pilot. Nero climbs in after me.

I still can't look at him.

"Here," he hands me a pair of huge headphones. "To block the sound."

I just stare at it blankly, still replaying the agony on that man's face.

Nero makes a noise of annoyance. He grabs the headset

back and reaches to place it on my head. The unexpected contact makes me flinch. I can't help it; I recoil from him like I've been stung.

Nero sees it. His jaw clenches, but he finishes positioning the earphones over my head. There's a microphone attached, too, and a moment later, his voice comes, scratchy through the headphones over the dull roar of the blades.

"You're judging me."

I still don't meet his eyes.

Nero snorts, his voice low and mocking. "What did you think my life looked like, Princess?"

He takes my jaw and turns my face to look at him dead-on. There's no escaping the shadows in his eyes, or the bitter edge to his voice as he continues: "The Barretti empire wasn't built on hugs and handshakes. Every day, I'm out there making choices that you could never dream about facing." Nero's eyes burn into me, full of loathing and fury. "You see the world in black and white, Princess, but in my world, there's nothing so simple. Everyone is covered in dirt, and blood, and shades of grey. *Everyone*," he growls. "There are no saints. And you can bet, some people deserve exactly what's coming to them."

I gulp. "People like that guy you were beating half to death?" I can't help asking. "Like my dad. Like *me*?"

Nero releases my jaw, and shakes his head, disdain clear on his face. He turns away from me and leans forward to say something to the pilot.

A moment later, we take off.

The flurry of noise and movement is a relief, surrounding me with something other than the dread taking root in my chest.

Focus, Lily, I remind myself. Nero's crimes won't help me now. The only thing that matters is helping him get close enough to Ian McKenna to lock down this vote of his. I can fake smiles and hand-holding for the weekend with the Devil himself if it lifts the death sentence hanging over Teddy and me.

Once Nero has his luxury development ready to go, I'll be free of him.

Forever.

SOON, we arrive at the lodge upstate, which is nestled in the countryside, surrounded by idyllic woods, fields, and a sparkling lake. I'm looking out at our surroundings when we arrive, and I get my first glimpse of the lodge. It's gorgeous.

Three stories tall, it's a log cabin-style building with a rough stone foundation, surrounded by smaller cabins dotted amongst the trees. The helicopter lands in a clearing nearby, and staff come out to get our luggage. I breath in the fresh air and notice that others are arriving in cars. I spot the McKennas emerging from one vehicle, and glance over at Nero. He's seen them too.

"Welcome to Stonybook," a hotel concierge greets us. "I have you in the Willow cabin, but we're gathering in the main lodge for refreshments, if you'd like to follow me."

We make our way into the lodge, and the stylishly rustic décor is the perfect blend of cozy and modern, with wood on the walls, a great stone fireplace, and lots of woven throws on the beat-up furniture.

I clock the décor and attitudes around us, and immediately peg it as old money: understated and fraying around the edges.

"The gentlemen are on the terrace," the concierge advises us.

Nero gives me a look. "You going to behave?" he asks in a low voice.

I narrow my eyes. "You're the one who needs to be on your

best behavior." I snap back. "Remember, no punching anybody's face in. It's not polite."

Nero strides off, and I breathe a sigh of relief to have some space between us. But it doesn't last long, not when I clock the other assembled wives and girlfriends, all greeting each other and sizing everyone up. We may be out in the country, but there's still plenty of designer jewelry and glossy hair on show, mixed with polished riding boots and casual khaki pants.

"Isn't this a hoot?" Marissa says, greeting me with a kiss on the cheek. "You must try the iced tea. Get it with a splash of bourbon," she adds with a wink. "It's going to be a long day."

Get your game face on.

"What a good idea. And I just love that scarf of yours!" I exclaim, beaming. "You must tell me where you got it from."

I chat with her as we head into the lounge. There's a sitting area with comfortable chairs and couches and a fireplace. A bookshelf against the walls is full of the classics and there's a piano near the window. There are six women here, all the significant others of men that are outside. Everyone is sipping tea and carrying on polite conversation, so I take a plate of snacks and find a seat close to Ian's wife, Fiona.

"A new face, how fun," the woman next to me says before I get a chance to initiate a conversation with Fiona. Marissa introduces me to everyone.

"Lily is one of my oldest friends," she says, smiling. "She's just back from Europe."

"Welcome. I'm Brittany," the woman beside me says, flipping back her red hair. She has porcelain skin and a faint Southern accent. "And my husband, Langdon, is probably making a fool of himself already. The poor man can't shoot straight."

The others laugh.

"Jerry would never admit it, but he's been practicing all month," another confides.

"It's the highlight of his social calendar," Brittany trills. She's young, in her mid-twenties, with model good looks and flawless makeup. The way she's dressed is a little more revealing than the other women, too, and there's an undercurrent of tension in the way her eyes dart around the room for approval.

She doesn't quite fit in among the others, but she's trying to. She must be here for a reason. It reminds me of Nero, and I make a mental note to keep an eye on her.

"So, will we be hunting, too?" I ask.

There's laughter.

"Oh, Lord, no," one of the older women says. "They have a fabulous spa here, so we like to take it easy."

"Leave the men to trample around in the mud," Fiona agrees with a smile. "I'm just happy to have the break."

"That's right," the doyenne says. "I remember the campaign trial, when my Harry was in the statehouse. It's a marathon."

Fiona nods. "Of course, I'm happy to support him," she says quickly.

"Of course," everyone echoes.

"But I have to say, I'm relishing the thoughts of a whole weekend away from his campaign team," she continues, "And the kids. It's the closest we've come to romance in forever!"

There's more laughter, but I notice, Brittany's eyes narrow at Fiona. It's just a glance, and she quickly masks it with a smile, but the hostility in her eyes takes me by surprise.

Interesting...

"Thank you for the hair tip, by the way," I say to Fiona, eager to establish a connection. "I tried the salon you mentioned, and it was amazing."

"Aren't they amazing?" she says. "Lily, wasn't it?"

I nod. "That's right." I angle my body closer. "I have to admit, I'm a little intimidated," I murmur, "My fiancée told me about this trip last-minute, but I'm not used to mixing in circles like this. I'm way over my head."

Fiona smiles understandingly. Because of course she does, my research showed that Fiona wasn't exactly born with a silver spoon in her mouth. She's from a small town in New Jersey and met Ian when she was in teacher training college. His meteoric rise in politics swept her into a new world, too, so I'm betting it'll help establish a bond to cast myself in the same light. "There's nothing to it," she reassures me. "Just relax, enjoy yourself—and watch Dolly over there after her fourth martini."

"I heard that!" Dolly calls, pink cheeked. Everyone is laughing good-naturedly, but Brittany purses her lips and takes another sip of her tea, shooting another barely-disguised glare at Fiona.

Yep, there's something here I need to investigate further.

AFTER ANOTHER HOUR OF CHIT-CHAT, everyone disperses to dress for dinner, and I find a staff member to show me to our cabin. The trail winds through the grounds, to a private spot beside a babbling brook. It would be romantic, if the man I was sharing it with wasn't a cold-blooded monster.

I open the door, preparing to relax before dinner, but when I step inside, Nero is already there.

Shirtless, his bare chest flexing as he rummages in one of the cases I packed.

"What are you doing here?" I blurt, thrown by the sight of him—and the proximity, the two of us alone in the cabin.

"What does it look like, Princess?" Nero buttons up a white

shirt, then strips off his jeans. I turn away, taking stock of the room while he dresses for dinner.

It's a luxury suite, done up in the same luxe rustic style as the main lodge, with a pair of deer antlers mounted on the wall and massive four-poster bed in the middle of the room, dominating the space.

The only bed, I realize with a sinking heart. I assumed there would be a living area, or some kind of couch one of us could sleep on, but there's no alternative.

No escape.

I gulp. "What are we going to do about the sleeping arrangements?" I ask. Nero is zipping up dress pants now, so it's safe to turn back.

As safe as I'll ever be, looking at him.

"What about them?" he asks.

I try not to blush. "There's only one bed."

Nero smirks. "You're not getting shy, are you? I've seen it all, sweetheart... Remember?"

Vividly.

I can't help but shiver at the memory of his body thrusting against mine. His hands, pinning me down. His mouth, taking me to heaven and back.

My cheeks burn hotter—and from the smug amusement on Nero's face, he can tell exactly what I'm thinking. He strolls towards me, and every nerve in my body freezes in anticipation for his touch as he reaches—

Past me. To the garment bag hanging by the door.

"Don't worry," Nero adds, his voice hard as ice. "I don't revisit past mistakes. Been there, done that. Or rather, I've done you."

Nero shrugs on a dinner jacket, and I feel a surge of humiliation.

"You're overdressing," I snap, taking a perverse pleasure in cutting him down in return for that statement. "Nobody will wear a suit to dinner. You'll stick out like a sore thumb."

I pull a more casual outfit from the closet, which the staff have already unpacked. "Jeans, casual button-down, a cashmere sweater," I instruct him. "Sneakers, too. I guessed your sizes."

He glowers at me but starts to strip out of the suit. I'm in no state for another show of his naked body, so I grab my own dinner outfit and head for the bathroom to change.

He moves to block my path.

"We'll be late," I protest, panic flaring at his closeness.

Panic, or something more dangerous.

Like desire.

But Nero doesn't move. "I'm getting tired of your attitude, Princess, acting like you're so far above me." He leans closer, his breath hot on my cheek. "You should remember, it's because of my generosity that you're still breathing. That your brother is still walking around out there. *Alive.*"

I swallow hard, my heart racing.

"You said you could be of value to me," he continues, eyes black and cold. "So don't forget—you need to earn your keep. And whether you do that at dinner, or in other ways... Well, that's up to you."

He trails a fingertip down my cheek, and I shiver, caught in the intensity of his gaze.

Other ways...

I can only guess what he's talking about. His finger trails lower, down my neck and over my collarbone, and I can't help shivering again.

Wanting him.

I wrench away, hating myself for my body's response. "I wouldn't ask you to demean yourself," I snap back, stepping around him. "After all, you said it yourself: It's time we both learned from our mistakes. Because loving you was the biggest mistake I ever made."

I head for the bathroom and slam the door—but not before I see the anger flash on Nero's face.

Anger, and something like hurt.

But that's impossible. A man like him isn't capable of feelings.

And the longer I remember that, the safer I'll be.

DINNER PASSES IN A BLUR. Ian and Fiona are seated at the other end of the big table, unfortunately, so I meet more people and try to keep all the names straight. It's a collection of financiers, politicos, and society types—the movers and shakers who really run the city behind the scenes. Nero and I are supposed to be an engaged couple, and I don't think much of that until we're seated together at the dinner table, and he drapes an arm around my shoulder, leaning in to kiss me on the cheek.

I tense, even though I'm in the middle of a conversation with Dahlia. Then, Nero leans close to my ear and whispers.

"Appearances, Princess. We're supposed to be in love."

Love. With the man I loathe to my core.

I force a smile, and snuggle closer to him, forcing a besotted smile. Go ahead and give me an Oscar, because this is the performance of my life, not grabbing the butter knife and stabbing it in his hand when he slowly begins tracing a circle on my bare shoulder.

The room shrinks to just that small point of contact, his touch hypnotic.

Turning me on.

Heat spirals through me. I want to pull away, but I already know, I can't. So, I just have to sit there through dinner, my body slowly going up in flames as he caresses me casually. Every inch the attentive fiancé.

"More wine, sweetheart?" he asks, brushing hair from my eyes.

"No, thank you," I reply. "You know what I'm like."

"I sure do." Nero chuckles, perfectly at ease, and that stubborn streak in me flares to life.

"Here, taste these berries," I coo, as dessert is served. "They're so ripe."

I pick up a perfect strawberry and bring it up to his lips, feeding him.

He shoots me a warning look, but I ignore it. I 'm not the only one who should suffer at this ruse.

"You always liked sweet things," I murmur, as I push the strawberry slowly through his lips, my fingertips grazing his mouth. His gaze darkens, flashing with fury, and pressed close against him, I feel his whole body tense as steel.

"See?" I purr. "Delicious."

I sit back, licking the juice from my fingers. Not breaking his gaze.

The air between us practically crackles with tension, but I refuse to back down and look away first.

He wanted PDA? I'll give him damn public displays of affection.

"Well!" There's an awkward laugh, and we both drag our eyes away to see people looking. "Guess who's in the honeymoon phase!"

"Can you blame me?" Nero says, relaxing back, all smiles again. "I mean, look at her."

I have to simper and smile, even as lust and rage whirl in a toxic cocktail in my chest. By the time we've finished eating, I'm exhausted keeping them both at bay. I manage polite 'goodnights,' and wordlessly follow Nero back to our cabin.

The minute the door shuts behind us, his amiable act drops. "Fuck," he curses, shoving a hand through his hair. "This whole event is bullshit. All that damn small talk, and I've barely said two words with McKenna. You said this would be my chance to get close," he adds, accusingly.

"We've been here a matter of hours," I say, exhausted, sitting on the edge of the bed and pulling off my heels. I rub the balls of my sore feet, wound way too tight for his attitude. "You don't forge a connection in a single day. You need to get to know people over time to build up trust. It takes patience. Something you're clearly lacking."

"Oh, I can be patient." Nero gives a cruel laugh. "I've been waiting years to make this development happen."

"Then what's another few days?" I retort. "You can't blame McKenna for being wary. All he knows is the Barretti name. You need to make him think you're more than that. Like he knows you."

"The way you made me believe I knew you?"

I look up. Nero is watching me with equal parts loathing and desire in his eyes.

The same feelings warring inside me, too.

"You knew me," I reply bitterly. "You knew me better than anyone."

"Don't lie," Nero growls. "There's nobody here to buy your innocent act."

I stare back at him, furious. Suddenly, our past isn't dead and buried, it's humming with life, right here in the confines of the cabin. Dangerous. *Hot*. It feels like I'm sixteen again, aching for him with an intensity I've never known before, despite my burning hatred.

Or because of it.

My body tightens. God, what would it feel like to have him

again? Scratch the itch that's been haunting me ever since the night I left? The possibility leaves me breathless.

No. Fuck. You can't.

I catch myself in time, and reel back. "I'm... Going to get some air," I blurt, before turning on my heel and fleeing the cabin.

Leaving Nero there, cursing my name.

12

LILY

I DON'T EVEN KNOW where I'm going as I leave the cabin. Back to the main lodge, I guess. Anything to delay the inevitable confrontation with Nero.

Anywhere to take a moment to breathe.

I make my way along the dark trail. There are lanterns lighting the way, but with the woods now dark around me, I feel the breeze on my bare shoulders and shiver.

The situation with Nero is set to combust. And even worse, a part of me wants it to.

I find the main lodge lit up. There aren't many people around, but I notice the bar area is open, and a couple of guys are drinking and having a murmured conversation in the corner. Some backroom deal, I'm sure, but that's the point of the whole weekend, isn't it?

I pour myself a shot of whiskey and sit on a bar stool. The alcohol burns going down, but it doesn't ease the tight ache in my chest.

Or between my thighs.

I'm so angry with myself, and I don't know how to handle

it. How can I still want him like this, knowing that he's truly a monster? I long for his hands to run over my body, but I saw those same hands beating a man half to death. Would he have stopped if I hadn't shown up?

How much blood does Nero already have on his hands?

I don't want to think about it. And I don't like feeling as if I have no control over my own body. It won't listen to reason, no matter how much my brain knows I should stay away.

I pour another shot, and linger at the bar, dreading going back to the cabin. Not because I can't bear to be around Nero.

But because of what I'm afraid I'll do, when I see him again.

Someone joins me at the bar. "Single malt? You've got the right idea."

I look up. It's one of the husbands from dinner: a man with dirty blonde hair and a dimple in his cheek. He's boyishly good-looking, and I remember he's here with an older-looking wife, someone dripping in jewelry.

"Mind if I...?" he asks, nodding to the bottle.

"Be my guest," I reply politely.

He pours a healthy measure for himself, then tops up my glass. "To the fine bartenders at Stonybrook," he says, with a twinkle in his eye. "You're Lily, right?"

"That's right," I say, surprised.

"Drew." He catches my look. "It's a skill of mine," he confides. "I can always remember a pretty face."

I shake my head, smiling despite myself. "Your compliments need work," I tell him. "Is your wife not joining you for a drink?" I add pointedly.

But he just grins. "She's conked out with a Valium," he says cheerfully. "Besides, the two of us are here for very different reasons."

"Is that so?"

"She's here to gossip with all her friends and get pampered at the spa, and I'm here to talk business. I have a very successful social media analytics company," he adds.

"And you're so modest, too." I toss back lightly. "She's a lucky woman."

He laughs, and I relax, able to imagine for a moment that I'm just hanging out at a regular bar, fending off the good-natured flirting of some random stranger.

Then an arm drapes around my shoulder. "There you are, Princess." Nero's voice comes, icy as hell. "I was worried you'd wandered off and gotten lost."

Fuck.

He eyes Drew with clear hostility. "I see you've met my fiancée," he says, drawing himself up to his full height. He couldn't have made it clearer that I'm his property if he'd pissed in a circle around me.

"I certainly have," Drew replies. "And what charming company she is."

Nero's grip tightens on my shoulder. "That's my Lily," he says, staring Drew down. The other man dips his head, as if recognizing Nero's dominance.

"Have a good night," he mutters, and retreats.

Nero yanks me to the door. "Time for bed, *sweetheart*." He says, loud enough for everyone to hear.

I have no choice but to follow him back to the cabin. But the second we're alone, I wrench away.

"What the hell was that?" I snap. "You're supposed to be making friends, not having a pissing contest with every man who looks at me. I'm not your property," I add, furious.

"Yes, you are." Nero growls. "As long as you're under my protection, playing at being my fiancée, *you belong to me!*"

I gape at the raw possession in his voice.

He angrily tears his shirt off and begins to undress, revealing the hard muscular planes of his chest.

I shiver at the sight. "Can you not do that in front of me?" I protest, my voice coming out high-pitched.

He just curls his lip in a cruel smirk. "What's the problem, Princess? I thought you liked to watch."

Oh God. The memory of him jacking off in the shower slams through me in a rush of heat and desire. But I'd rather die than let him know just how much it turned me on, so I raise my chin and sneer.

"You can keep the show to yourself. The preview didn't exactly whet my appetite, if you know what I mean. Besides, you said it yourself, we've both been there, done that. Although, it's all kind of hazy, when I think about it," I can't help adding. "Guess it wasn't so memorable for me."

The moment the words are out of my mouth, I know I've pushed him too far. All amusement vanishes from Nero's features and is replaced with something dark, almost predatory.

"Bullshit."

He takes a step forward. I take a step back. My mouth is dry and my heart is pounding, but still, I force myself to give a careless shrug. "It was nothing. We were kids. I'm sure you did the best you could, at the time."

Nero gives a sharp laugh. "That what you've been telling your-self, Princess? When you're laying in bed late at night, rubbing that sweet clit of yours, we both know I'm the only one on your mind."

Heat spirals through me. Heat—and shame.

How does he know?

Nero's smile grows, stalking closer. "Yeah, I thought so. When those fingers are moving faster, and you're whimpering for more, I'm the one you want, aren't I, Princess? It's my hands you want, pinning you to the mattress. My cock you need, filling that tight cunt all the to the fucking limit. Because you know damn well, you've never had it so good."

Oh my God.

"But as good as those memories are, you're forgetting one thing, Princess," Nero growls, taking another step closer. "I'm not a fucking kid anymore. I'm all man."

There's silence for a moment, our eyes locked. The air thick with sex.

Then he lunges for me, and our mouths lock in a red-hot inferno of a kiss.

Fuck.

It's been building so long between us, I couldn't have stopped it if I tried. His lips are hard on mine, punishing and ravenous as he slams me back against the wall. I melt into it, returning the kiss, but he immediately takes control. Licking his way into my mouth, he roams his hands all over my body, igniting a fire in my blood.

God, he still knows everything I like as he grips the back of my neck, his fingers tangled in my hair. I moan into his mouth, desperately writhing closer as his free hand finds my breast, his thumb running over the hardened bud of my nipple through my thin dress. Our tongues tangle as he pins me against the wall, trapped there and oh, so willing.

My palms land on his chest, feeling the hard muscle and trailing up until my arms are wrapped around his neck. I can barely catch my breath as he leaves bruising kisses on my lips, bucking his hard body against me, leaving me damp and mewling, arching up for more.

"That's right," he growls, nipping at my neck, thrusting his thick length between my thighs. "Beg for it, baby. We both know you want to."

But I bite my lip, the last part of my brain refusing to give him what he wants. Nero lets out a harsh chuckle, squeezing at my nipple again. "Not there just yet? Don't worry. You will be."

His hand moves down, skimming over my ribcage as his other grabs my wrists and pins them up above my head, immobilizing me. He hikes up my dress and presses his fingers between my thighs against my panties, right over my clit.

I moan, legs shaking.

"I remember," Nero growls. "I remember how you like it. Right here, baby. Just like that."

He rubs me through the silk, agonizingly slow. I writhe, trying to press against his touch, but he keeps me pinned in place, tongue trailing over my sensitive neck as he slowly circles my clit through the damp fabric.

"Fuck," he groans against my skin. "So fucking wet. I bet you've been dripping since dinner. Yeah, I saw it written all over your face, the way you wriggled in your seat."

"You were hard, too," I gasp, head thrown back in pleasure. "Don't think I didn't know."

Nero growls angrily, tugging my panties aside and sinking two fingers inside me so fast, I cry out at the thick, sweet intrusion.

Oh my god!

He pumps into me, thrusting deep, and I cry again, my voice echoing in the dark room. Fuck, it feels so good. I can't think, I can't breathe, all that matters is what he's doing to me right now.

"You like that, Princess?" he demands, his voice gruff in my ear.

I whimper, clenching around his fingers, grinding against his palm.

"I thought so." Nero pumps faster. "Look at you, taking my fingers like a greedy girl. Not too good for me now, are you? It must kill you to know that a man like me can make you feel so fucking good."

He's right, and it only makes this hotter: shame and lust and loathing rising in my body, driving me to the edge. He angles his fingers, pausing to rub my inner walls, seeking, searching for—

"Nero!" I cry, pleasure slamming through me. "Fuck! Right there!"

I raise up on my tiptoes, chasing the rush. But his fingers still.

"Beg for it."

My eyes snap open. Nero is watching me, jaw set.

"I..."

"Beg for it, Princess." His eyes are dark, fixed on mine. "I'll give it to you, baby. You know I'll take you all the way. But if you want to come, I need to hear that pretty mouth of yours beg for what you need."

He strokes again, just once, and I whimper. So close to release. So damn close...

Fuck. I'm too far gone to stop now.

"Please!" I cry, hating myself and thrilling in the surrender all at the same time. "Please, Nero! I need you!"

His eyes flash with victory, and then his fingers are working their magic again: Rubbing deep and swift inside me as his palm grinds my clit and makes me see stars.

My orgasm slams through me, and I come apart with a scream, my fingers digging into his shoulders as I revel in the most epic orgasm I can remember.

Holy shit.

I sag back against the wall, reeling. I'm dazed, gasping for air when I realize that Nero has torn away from me. I catch a glimpse of sheer loathing on his face as he turns and heads for the door. Then it slams behind him, and I'm left alone.

My legs give way, and I collapse to the floor, my body still humming with pleasure. But my mind? It's already full of doubts. It's clear Nero regrets everything that just happened. That he still hates me.

The worst part is, even knowing that—even knowing him— I want *more*.

13

NERO

I SLIP the night manager a hundred bucks, and sleep in a free room up at the lodge. I told him me and the missus had a disagreement, but despite the swanky surroundings, I barely sleep, hearing Lily's whimpers of pleasure echoing in my mind.

Another moment, another plea, and I would have given her exactly what she needed: My cock buried deep in that sweet, needy cunt, fucking her so good she would never pretend to forget me again.

Because we both know, that was a lie. She remembers, alright.

The problem is that I do too.

Nothing was ever as good as the way she spread her legs for me all those years ago, clutching on and moaning while I tried my hardest to make it last. The way she made me feel, sinking inside her untouched pussy for the first time... like a goddamn warrior.

Like a God.

I've been craving it for a decade now, and I was inches away from quenching my thirst last night. Fucking her up against the wall and driving deep, making her scream the fucking walls down. Proving once and for all, I'm not an eager kid anymore.

Inch by hard, throbbing inch.

So what stopped me?

It's the question I'm still asking myself, hard and sleepless, all night long. By dawn, I need to get myself together, so I head down to the pool. Over the years, I've learned that physical exercise is a good way to keep myself under control. My urges, mostly sex and violence, can be curbed by working it all out of my system.

The problem is that I've been swimming laps for an hour now, pushing myself beyond exhaustion, but I still want Lily so much that I think I might lose my mind over it.

At this point, I feel like I'm punishing myself to escape my desire. But there is no escape. Even when she was gone in Vegas or wherever the hell she was all those years, I wanted her.

Dreamed about her.

Closed my eyes and pictured her face with every other woman I fucked.

Coming to the edge of the pool, I pull myself up onto it, sitting and trying to catch my breath. Did she catch a wink of sleep either? I doubt it. She probably hates herself for letting me put my hands on her. We both know, they're stained with blood that will never wash out.

Fuck, it was written all over her face, when she saw me beating that guy back in the city. The shock. The disgust. She thinks I'm a monster for all the sins to my name.

She's right.

I am.

"Mr. Barretti?"

I turn. It's the concierge. "I thought you should know; the

gentlemen are gathering soon."

I nod harshly. "Thanks for the warning."

Reluctantly, I grab a robe and head back to the cabin. To my relief, she's already dressed and gone, so I can quickly rinse off and dress without her temptation right there, taunting me.

But I don't know what I'm going to do tonight. I feel too out of control when I'm alone with her, like I'm capable of anything.

And Lily feels it too. Even with my fingers buried deep inside her, I could see the resentment in her eyes. She hates the way I make her feel, that her body responds to me so powerfully.

Yeah, well take a number, sweetheart. That makes two of us.

I MAKE my way to the lobby to find McKenna and the other men, but as usual, my eyes go straight to Lily. It's always been like that. I've always been able to find her in a crowd. It's like my body and mind are so in tune with her that I always sense when she's in my orbit. She's chatting with some of the other women, looking breezy and effortless in linen pants and a tank top. Polished and perfect.

They would never guess she was begging me so sweetly just a few hours ago, clenching her cunt around my fingers like a goddamn vice.

She meets my eyes across the room and quickly looks away. She can't even look at me.

"Woah, someone got out on the wrong side of bed!" one of the guys joke, seeing my stormy expression.

I grab a Thermos of coffee from the table and remind myself: I'm here for a reason. And it's not biting the head off every rich asshole around.

Eyes on the prize, motherfucker.

"Let's get this show on the road."

It's a small group, just four of us. We take a couple of ATVs out into the woods, parking them in a small clearing and walking the rest of the way to the trap, in the trees. As we settle in with our rifles, I make sure that I'm positioned next to McKenna. It's the first time I've gotten near him so far, and I need to make it count.

"Nice day for it," he says, friendly, as we unpack our binoculars and breakfast.

"Uh huh," I murmur. Then I remember everything Lily's been preaching at me, about building a connection. Social bullshit isn't my style, but if that's what it takes to secure this real estate deal, then fuck it, I'll make small talk all day long.

"It's a great spot," I continue, "Have you been coming out to the lodge long?"

McKenna nods, digging into the breakfast sandwiches the chef prepared for us. "A few years now. You know, it was Rex over there who talked me into my City Council run, right here on one of these trips."

He points out Rex, a paunchy older guy, set up in the other trap.

I hide a snort. Backroom deals, movers and shakers. Sounds about right.

"What about you?" McKenna asks, eying me curiously. "What brings you out to the woods this year?"

A certain cash payment to one of the founders of this getaway, buying my spot in the lodge. But of course, I'm not going to tell him that.

"Oh, you know, seemed like a good opportunity to widen my circle," I reply. "Plus, it's nice to get away from the city, get some fresh air."

"I agree," McKenna says. "Something about being in

nature, really puts everything in perspective. You're in the transport industry, aren't you?"

"Sure am," I reply, even though we both know that's just the Barretti cover. "Shipping, trucking, logistics... But I'm branching out into real estate now."

"Are you?" McKenna plays it cool, looking through his binoculars. "Interesting."

"Building a better New York. Isn't that what we're all aiming for?"

"True enough."

One of the other guys hushes us, already on his stomach with his rifle scope primed. "C'mon, quiet. You'll scare them away."

McKenna shoots me a grin and rolls his eyes. "Yes, *mom*," he says, and takes up position. I follow suit, even though I couldn't care less about the hunt.

The real prey is right beside me.

We wait in silence for a while, which is broken when a text alert sounds.

"C'mon!" the serious guy complains. "What are we doing here?"

"Sorry!" McKenna pull the phone out of his pocket and checks it. He sighs when he sees what's on the screen.

"Work trouble?" I ask.

"I wish," he says, turning the phone off. "At least that I could solve. But women..."

I give a friendly chuckle. "I swear to God, you can't live with 'em."

"Aren't you here with that blonde?" McKenna asks. "My wife was talking about her. Lily, wasn't it?"

"Uh huh," I try to look like a loved-up schmuck. "I swear, she has me wrapped around her finger."

McKenna sighs. "Be careful, that's when the problems start. When you're so crazy for her, you get sloppy."

I pause. It's a weird thing to say from a man who's been married fifteen years. But before I can dig deeper, there's a scratch of static on the walkie-talkie, and a voice comes.

"Approaching."

We all lower our rifles as an ATV drives up, and an earnest looking guy climbs out. "Councilman."

"Keith?" McKenna looks surprised. "What are you doing out here? This is my chief of staff," he adds, introducing him.

"I'm sorry," Keith says. "But you're needed back in the city. The mayor just saw your housing report, and, well... He wants to meet at four. I have a car ready."

McKenna sighs. "Fiona's just going to love this," he tells me ruefully. "Sorry to bow out early, gentlemen. Enjoy the rest of the trip."

He climbs onto the ATV, and then he's gone. Back to the city—and away from any chance to bond with the guy.

Dammit.

I STICK it out another hour before calling it a day, too, and head back to the lodge. My temper is growing. This whole damn weekend has been a bust. Nothing but an exercise in futility.

And blue balls.

I find Lily sitting at the pool with the other women. I notice she's talking to some other young woman, laughing and chatting as she lays out in the sun. It looks way too much like she's really on a weekend retreat. It's like she belongs here and is having fun.

Is this all just a game to her?

When she sees me, she must read something in my expression because she cuts her conversation short and comes to join me.

"What's going on?" she asks. Her hand starts to reach out for me, but she stops before making contact, closing her fist and lowering it to her side.

She can't bring herself to touch me, even to keep up appearances in front of the group.

Ice settles in my veins.

"We're leaving." I growl.

She frowns. "Why?"

"McKenna's gone. Heading back to the city."

Her face clears. "Oh, that must be why Fiona disappeared."

"So, game's up," I say curtly. "No point prolonging this bullshit for no good reason."

She swallows, looking away. "Fine with me."

The staff pack our things and take us out to the helicopter pad to meet out ride. We climb aboard and take off, making the short ride back to the city without another word.

Without me even glancing at her.

I can sense Lily's confusion. A couple of times, she even makes a comment, looking to me for a response. I don't give it to her.

I can't.

Because this is a dangerous game I'm playing, even keeping her close. I'm risking my power and position just keeping her alive. What happened last night can't happen again. It was a moment of weakness, and I won't be weak again.

Lily doesn't belong in my world. My bloody hands have no place on her body.

She's good for one thing, and one thing only:

To get me McKenna's vote.

And after that?

She's nothing to me again.

14

LILY

SOMETHING CHANGED between me and Nero at the lodge. Or maybe it just went back to the way things were when I was first brought to him, when he was so cold and angry, vengeance burning in his eyes.

I thought maybe we'd started to move past that. I wouldn't have said we were friends, but begrudging partners at the very least.

Now, it's all icy silence in the apartment. He won't talk to me unless he absolutely has to, and even then, it's clipped and confrontational.

It's probably stupid of me to be surprised by that, but I can't lie to myself. After things heated up out in the country, a small part of me hoped that was going to happen again. That we could at least find common ground in this chemistry between us.

Scratch the itch that's driving me crazy, just being around the man.

But that would be a monumental mistake. So maybe it's better that he's radiating disdain and fury every time we pass each other by in the hall. But as the week passes, my restlessness grows. I'm trapped here with him, and the tension is only building. There's no ignoring his presence in this apartment, which leaves me plagued with desire that has no outlet. And with nothing on the McKenna's social calendar that I can find, it leaves me with nothing on my mind but Nero.

His body. His business.

The FBI.

When my phone rings on Friday, I'm so desperate for a distraction, that I snatch it up, despite the unknown number.

"Lily? Hi! It's Juliet."

Juliet? I scour my brain for a face to go with the name. Then, it hits me. The woman from the ballet, the one that Nero was actually nice to.

His sister-in-law, technically.

"Oh, hi," I say, not sure how to react to this unexpected development.

"I was wondering if you'd like to have lunch with me today." Juliet says, friendly. "Just a casual bite, Francine's, around noon?"

"Yes!" I blurt. Anything to get out of here for a few hours. And get away from him. "I mean, that sounds great," I add, more casual. "See you there."

I hang up, wondering how she got my number. And why she would want to get to know someone on Nero's arm. They seemed friendly, but still, the Barretti name is usually radioactive, and the Sterlings... Well, they're about as high society as they come.

Either way, it'll be a distraction from my captivity, so I happily dress and let my stony-faced driver-slash-prison guard, Kyle, take me to the restaurant.

When I walk in, Juliet's already at the best table. She bobs up and greets me with genuine enthusiasm.

Which only makes my curiosity grow.

"I have to ask," I say, when we've settled in and placed our orders. "How did you get my number?"

"I asked Nero," Juliet says with a smile.

I blink. "So, you guys are... Friends?" I ask, confused. Because there's nothing about this that makes sense. Juliet is sweet and smart, and doesn't seem like the kind of woman to be palling around with a violent mob boss.

"I wouldn't say that," she gives a wry grin. "But we've reached an... Understanding. After all, we are family."

"Family?" I repeat, even more confused.

Juliet's eyes widen. "He didn't tell you?"

My expression clearly answers for me.

"Maybe I shouldn't say anything..." she backs off. "But, since you guys are engaged... Nero and my husband, Caleb, are brothers," she confides. "Half-brothers, through Nero's father."

"Roman." I say, my mind blown.

"They only found out recently," Juliet adds. "And it's kind of a touchy subject. They're not exactly on the best terms. Yet." She says, sounding determined. "But I'm working on it."

I shake my head, absorbing the news. "Wow. That's... Wow."

"I hope it's OK to tell you," Juliet pauses. "Since you're joining the family, too."

"Right," I blurt. The fake engagement.

Juliet's gaze moves to my hand, and she frowns when she sees there's no ring on my finger. "Did he not give you a ring? I swear to God, some men—"

"No, it's okay," I interrupt, thinking that if this charade goes on too much longer, I'll have to get Nero to buy me a rock. Although, for some reason I can't explain, I don't like the idea of that. It makes it feel too real. "It's at the jewelers, getting resized."

"Oh, okay." She smiles. "I'm a *big* jewelry fan. Comes from spending all that time at Sterling Cross. But we should talk about the real reason I invited you here." she pushes her plate aside and fixes me with a serious look.

Fuck. My heart sinks. Not more ulterior motives.

"I need to know everything about you and Nero," Juliet lightens into a grin. "How did this happen? I thought nobody would climb those stony walls of his."

Gossip. That's all. She wants girl-talk and gushing.

I exhale in relief.

"How did you guys meet?" Juliet prompts me eagerly.

"We actually had a thing years ago," I say slowly, figuring a version of the truth is best. Juliet seems so nice, I don't want to spin a wild story for her. "I moved away for a while, but since I've been back, we've rekindled things."

"How romantic," she beams.

I can't help flashing a wry look. "Well, that's not to say things aren't... Complicated."

Juliet smiles. "I know a few things about complicated."

Does she? My skepticism must show, because she pauses, assessing me again.

"Lily, I know I'm just a stranger but, I'd like to be your friend. And if you ever need to talk..."

I nod and give her a closed lip smile. "Thanks."

I appreciate her offer, but I know I can't ever reveal the truth. Besides, what could I say? "The man I loved is threatening me with death in revenge for my father's betrayal, so now I have to pretend to the world I'm happy with him just to make it through the week'?

Not exactly girl-talk for lunch and bubbles, is it?

I don't want to talk about Nero anymore, so I change to the subject to movies and TV shows. I've had more free time on my hands lately since I'm stuck in Nero's apartment ninety percent of the time. The only saving grace has been that the man has every streaming service available. I've wasted way too many hours binging TV shows, but at least I'm up to date on the latest reality shows, and soon we're gossiping about wild dating programs and new books.

"This was so much fun," Juliet says, after we bicker over who gets to pay the bill and make our way to the exit. "Let's do it again soon."

"Sure," I lie. I could see Juliet becoming a friend if things were different. If I were going to stick around.

If I were really with Nero.

We're on our way out when we pass a group of women just entering the restaurant. I recognize one of them, it's Brittany, the redhead from the hunting retreat.

The one who has a problem with Fiona McKenna.

"Brittany?" I pause to greet her, pasting on a big smile.

"Lily? Oh, my God, what are the chances of running into each other?" she says, hugging me like we're sisters instead of women that spent a single day together last weekend. "These are some of my old sorority sisters."

She rattles off names, and I don't retain a single one. It doesn't matter. I introduce Juliet.

"That's a beautiful necklace," Juliet compliments her. "I recognize it from the Spring line."

"You are sooo lucky, having the whole store at your disposal," Brittany sighs. "I actually have an account there. I just pick whatever I want and my special someone picks up the tab." She winks, and I wonder if her special someone is her husband—or someone else.

"Brittany, are we going to eat or what?" one of her sorority sisters interrupts.

"I'd better go," Brittany says. "I'll see you later. And I'll see you at the store soon, no doubt," she adds to Juliet with a laugh.

We exit the restaurant. "Friend of yours?" Juliet asks.

"Yeah, nope," I reply. "Although clearly she's a friend to Sterling Cross." Then I'm struck with a thought. "Does Nero have an account there, too?"

Juliet pauses, looking reluctant. "Yes."

I shouldn't be surprised. Of course he buys expensive jewelry, to lavish on his dates. "Anyone in particular shopping on it?"

Juliet pauses again.

"It's OK," I lie. "I just want to know what I'm dealing with."

She sighs. "There is one woman," she admits. "Avery, I think her name is. She always picks up things."

I frown, remembering Avery from that first meeting I overheard. She's loyal and beautiful. Oh, and one of Nero's oldest friends. At least, that was what he told me about her, back in the day.

Jealousy stabs through me.

"Don't worry about it," Juliet says, and I can tell that she feels guilty for saying anything at all. "I'm sure it means nothing. I mean, lots of men have their secretaries come in to pick out gifts and jewelry for them. They really need the help."

"Right," I agree, with a light laugh. "I should be thanking her."

Except for one thing. Avery isn't Nero's secretary.

We say our goodbyes, and Juliet heads back to the store. I know that I should call Kyle to come get me, but I'm not ready to do that yet. I need time to think, and I need to walk because I'm burning with jealousy, and I don't think I can sit still while I feel that way.

So, I head uptown, wondering about the relationship between Nero and Avery and trying to tell myself that I shouldn't care.

It doesn't matter. He doesn't belong to me. Why should I care who he's buying expensive jewelry for?

Except I do.

I turn a corner, only to feel a hand clamp down on my arm. I let out a small shriek as a man starts to drag me, with a force I'm powerless to fight, toward a white van sitting at the curb.

What the hell?

I try to scream, but a hand covers my mouth as I'm thrown inside the vehicle. Everything turns upside-down, and by the time I get my bearings, the door is slammed shut behind me.

Fuck.

I twist around on the metal floor of the van. I'm still disoriented by the sudden attack, when I feel a hand on my arm, I scream, "No!"

"Lily, calm down."

It's the calmness of the voice that makes me stop and pay attention. It's so out of place in a situation like this. Plus, he knows my name.

I blink a couple of times and see Agent Greggs sitting across from me.

And just like that, my day gets even worse.

15

LILY

I'M USHERED in a freight elevator up to a room on the fifth floor of a hotel. Just me and three super-conspicuous FBI agents in their black suits and earpieces.

The minute I'm led into a conference room, I whirl on Agent Greggs.

"Are you out of your fucking mind?" I demand. "What if Nero or even one of his men saw you take me? If he finds out that I've even spoken to the FBI, he'll think I'm betraying him, and I'll wind up dead! Did you even think of that?"

"Sit down, Lily," he tries to calm me.

"I will not fucking sit!" I scream. I complied at the first meeting, but I'm not playing along now. I'm too angry. "This is my life on the line!"

Agent Greggs looks uneasy. "We know. That's why we staged the grab. If anyone saw, it's clear that you were taken against your will."

"Like that will help me," I snap back.

I start to pace, my nerves going haywire. One illicit meeting was bad enough, but this?

If Nero finds out, I'm dead for sure.

And my brother...

I shiver in fear. "What do you want? I told you, I have nothing to say to you."

"And we both know, that's a lie," Agent Greggs replies. "You know exactly who it is you're living with. Nero Barretti is no innocent—and neither are you. But whatever hold he has over you, we can help," he urges. "Let us protect you."

Protection.

"Out of the kindness of your heart?" I shoot back, my voice laden with scorn. I may not trust Nero, but I don't trust the Feds, either.

"No," Agent Greggs admits. "In exchange for testimony. Information that can put Nero behind bars—where he belongs. Like father, like son."

"You mean, like father, like *daughter*," I correct him, reminded of my own father's choice to sell out the Barrettis. He may have thought he was doing what he needed to protect his family back then, but it didn't exactly turn out the way he planned.

"Come on, Lily," Greggs says to me, laying his hands flat on the conference table. "Work with me on this. Whatever you want, we can make it happen."

I take a breath and try to get a grip on my emotions. I'm caught in the middle here, stuck between Nero and the Feds.

I need to play it smart if I'm going to make it through unscathed. Make Greggs think there's at least the possibility of me playing ball.

I force myself to sit back in the chair, like I'm relaxing. "You want to know what I need? I'd like some water," I say finally.

"Of course." Greggs glances at one of the other suits, who quickly grabs one from the mini fridge.

"Thank you." I take a slow sip, my mind racing. If Agent

Greggs has gone through the trouble of staging that whole kidnap scene just to speak to me again, he must really need me —and whatever information he thinks I can provide.

That means I have value to him. Just like I found a way to have value to Nero.

"You wanted to talk?" I say, looking to him expectantly. "Talk."

Agent Greggs looks relieved, like half the battle is won. "We want you to gather intel on Nero Barretti. You're inside his apartment, you have access to his schedule and devices. You can pass important information back to us, help build our case against him."

"You want me to narc," I say flatly.

"Inform," Greggs corrects me, like the word choice makes any difference. It's all the same thing.

Betrayal.

"Your father worked for us, just like this." Greggs adds. "He stepped up, he did the right thing, and I know he'd want you to do the same thing."

"Would he?" I give a bitter laugh. "I'm not so sure about that. Do you know what it's like to go into witness protection? To lose everything you have in life, everything you've worked for, in an instant? I woke up one morning to find out that I was being ripped away from everything I knew. And for what?" I ask. "To lock up one man?"

"We are fighting against violent criminals here," Greggs says, and I can tell his patience is wearing thin. "Your father became our informant because he knew that Roman was a dangerous man doing terrible things. The Barretti organization has its reach in the worst this city has to offer: drugs, gambling, weapons," Greggs ticks them off. "And Nero is the one in charge now. It's on his head, every last crime."

I don't reply.

One of the other agents hands over a brown folder. Greggs tosses it onto the table in front of me.

I don't want to look at what's inside. I'm sure about that. It's not going to be good.

But I have to. I need to know everything I can so that I can decide what to do.

I finally flip open the folder, only to let out a sharp gasp at the picture I see. I recoil back, so Greggs reaches across the table and spreads out all five pictures on the table so I have no choice but to look at them.

At the mangled body of a man, laying dead on a garbage heap.

I feel bile rise up in my throat, and I have to look away.

"W-what is this?" I croak. My hands are shaking.

"Some poor bastard that got on the wrong side of the Barrettis." Greggs replies. "We found him by the river. This is what he looked like before they got a hold of him."

He pulls another picture out of the folder. This time it's a head shot, and as I take in his face, my blood runs cold.

Oh my God.

It's the man, the one I saw Nero beating half to death at his office.

"*Finish the job.*" Nero's calm instruction echoes in my head.

I think I'm going to be sick.

"Look at these pictures. This is who you're protecting."

"You think Nero did this?" I ask, trying not to show emotion. "Why don't you arrest him?"

Greggs pauses. "We don't have any evidence it was him, directly. But just because it wasn't his finger on the trigger, it doesn't mean he didn't order the hit. An innocent man is dead. Is that who you want to protect?"

The question lingers. But Greggs doesn't know that it's not

Nero I'm protecting with my silence, it's my brother and myself.

I get to my feet. "I want to leave."

"We're not finished yet."

"I'm sorry, I wasn't clear." I move to the door. "I *am* leaving, right now."

The two male FBI agents are standing in front of me, blocking my way. My heart beats faster with fear, but I refuse to show any weakness. "Is this how you plan to convince me to help you? By holding me hostage until I agree?"

After another moments, the agents move aside.

But Greggs goes after me, following into the hallway. "Think about it, Lily," he says, as I stride to the elevator. "Do you want the next body to be yours? Or Teddy?"

His question follows me, as I board the elevator on shaky legs. I get down to the lobby, and hurry from the hotel, blindly walking block after block, trying to put distance between me and what just happened. Those terrible photos. But I already know, no matter how far I get, I won't be able to erase the awful pictures burned into my brain.

If Greggs wanted to shock me, it worked.

But that doesn't mean I trust him. If anything, it's a grim reminder just how high the stakes for my family really are.

I see a convenience store and go inside. There are prepaid cell phones on the shelf, and I pick one at random. It's risky to use Nero's credit card to buy it, but I don't have any money of my own right now. All I can hope is that he won't pay too much attention to single convenience store charge when I've spent thousands on clothes and designer accessories already.

I need to talk to my brother right now—and I can't call him on the cell phone Nero gave me—so I take the burner phone and walk a couple of blocks to a small park, finding a private spot on a bench to make the call.

The phone rings three times before my brother answers.

"Hello?" his voice is guarded, and I realize it's because he doesn't recognize the phone number. He probably thinks it's a telemarketer.

"Hey kid, it's me."

"Lily?" His voice relaxes. "Hey, where have you been? You haven't been responding to my texts."

"Yeah, sorry about that. Dropped my phone in the toilet," I lie.

"So, is this your new number?"

"No, I borrowed a phone from a friend. I'll buy a new one soon."

The lies just keep spilling out and I hate that I can't be honest with him. But this is how it has to be.

"What are you up to?" Teddy asks. "You sound weird."

"I do?" I try to force my voice back to normal. "That's just because I'm tired. You know how it is the day after a late shift at the club."

"I don't like that you work there."

"Don't worry about me," I say, somehow managing to keep my voice light. "A shitty job isn't the end of the world. Now, tell me about you. How are your classes going?"

He launches into a detailed answer about every class he's taking, the study buddies and professors, and his dorm's plans for Prank Week. I listen to it all with a smile on my face, glad at the innocent distraction from everything I've been going through. He's so full of life and hope. None of the ugliness that I'm dealing with should ever touch him.

"Just remember to keep your grades up with all this fun you're having," I tease him lightly.

"I will! Plus..." Teddy pauses. "Well, there's a girl."

"A girl? Wow. Look at you," I cheer. "My brother, the stud."

"Shut up, it's not like that. She's really great."

Teddy has always been a little shy, but as he tells me about her, I can hear the excitement in his voice. He's smitten.

For some reason, this makes me feel even more afraid.

He's on the edge of greatness, at a point where he can do anything with his life. He could marry this girl, have a family. He could have an amazing career.

He could be happy.

I feel a lump in my throat. That's what is at stake here. Teddy's life. My life. All of it.

"Listen, I have to run to class," he finally says. "Check in next week? And remember to give me your number. You're missing out on some truly great viral videos, being off the grid."

"I promise," I tell him, trying to keep back the tears. "Be safe!"

I hang up, and sit there for a long moment, watching the city bustle by.

I miss Teddy so much it hurts, but I know what I have to do to protect the both of us. The FBI wants me to be an informant, but I know from experience, there's no safety in that. More witness protection, always looking over our shoulders, always waiting for the day Nero walks through the door.

He's a force of nature. A hurricane.

And he always gets what he wants.

So, I won't bet against him. There's nobody smarter or more ruthless. And if the Feds had any real chance of busting him, they wouldn't need me. He's given me his word that if I land him this deal, Teddy and I will be free. Safe. Forever.

Nobody else can give me that kind of security.

But if he finds out I've been talking to the Feds... If I fail to deliver, or if the FBI busts him on something and I go down with him...

There's danger everywhere I look. All I can do is hope I'm making the right choice.

And pray to God, Nero keeps his word.

My phone buzzes with a call—Nero's phone. And it's him calling.

I feel a surge of panic. Has he heard about the meet?

Images of the dead man flash in my mind as I pick up, cautious. "Hello?"

"Where are you?" he demands.

I gulp. "I just... Took a walk after lunch, to get some air."

"Get back soon," he orders me. "There's another fancy gala event tonight, McKenna's supposed to make an appearance, so we need to do the dog-and-pony show."

I let out a breath of relief. He doesn't know. "Fine. I'm on my way."

I hang up and try to steel myself for the night ahead on his arm. Because as tough as this façade has been so far, it's only getting harder.

And I need to give the performance of a lifetime.

16

LILY

I FEEL like I'm on autopilot as I attend the gala that evening. I can't stop thinking about those disturbing pictures and I feel guilty, even though that's insane. What could I have possibly done to stop that man from being killed? I have no power over Nero. I'm useful to him, that's all.

Despite my plan to continue on this path, I feel haunted by what I've seen. Greggs' words keep replaying in my mind.

Do you want to be the next body?

Or your brother?

This gala has a silent auction and we're circling the tables with high-dollar items. Trips to Europe, dining at the chef's table at a five-star restaurant, and even a boat. Nero remains pleasant, smiling on cue, and acting like the doting fiancé.

He's getting better at the act, just like me. He barely even flinches when we touch.

A waiter walks by with a tray of champagne, and I turn to grab a glass. Being a little tipsy tonight certainly won't be a bad thing. But then my eyes land on Ian McKenna standing on the other side of the room. His wife, Fiona, is nowhere to be seen, but I've picked up on the fact that he's a social butterfly, so this isn't surprising.

What has caught my attention is that he's talking to Brittany. They aren't touching or even standing too close to each other, but there's something about the look in her eyes as she gazes up at him.

It's like she has stars in her eyes.

And Ian? Well, he's not exactly keeping his distance. He leans closer to murmur something, and Brittany tosses her head back to laugh. Their eyes lock, just for a moment, and then they move an appropriate distance apart again, but that one glimpse was enough.

Suddenly, everything clicks into place.

I think about the weird vibe I picked up on when I first met Brittany at the hunting lodge. She definitely has an issue with Fiona, whatever she might smile.

Jealousy, perhaps? And guilt... For sleeping with her husband.

It would make sense. It also explains Brittany's comment about a special someone buying her jewelry. If that was her husband, she wouldn't need to be cagey about it. But if it's Ian McKenna, beloved politician...

Well, that's a different story.

I tug Nero's arm. "Let's get some air," I say meaningfully. I steer us to a small courtyard, away from the crowd.

"What is it?" Nero tenses, just being alone with me.

"I think I might have something..." I fill him in on my suspicions. "I know it's not much to go on, but I have an instinct. There's a weird vibe going on."

Nero doesn't say anything, but he looks thoughtful.

"Is it useful?" I ask, wanting to remind him I'm here for a reason.

"Could be. I'll look into it."

I can't help feeling disappointed, but I let it go. I'll just have to keep watching those two for more signs that I'm right.

The gala drags on, and Nero gets a small opportunity to talk to McKenna. This time, he seems to have listened to me: The guys chat about sports, and cars, and nothing remotely related to work. I even see McKenna laugh and slap Nero's back over something.

Progress. Thank God.

"You know what I don't understand?" Nero asks me as a waiter stops by with a tray of stuffed mushrooms. "Why do they schedule these things during dinner hours, then serve these pretentious little bites?"

I agree. "You remember the sausage and mushroom pizza we used to get at Rowdy's?" I ask.

I swear something softens in Nero's eyes as he looks at me. I wonder if he's remembering all the good times we had at our favorite pizza place, back when we were sneaking around. We must have spent hours hiding out in the back booth, splitting a pie with extra cheese, talking about everything under the sun.

Nero puts his champagne glass down on the table. "You know what? Let's go get some real food."

I DON'T BELIEVE the old pizza joint will still be standing until we walk through the doors and the memories hit me.

"I can't believe that nothing has changed about this place!" I exclaim. I look around at the exposed brick walls and eclectic collection of tables and chairs. There's a wood-fire pizza oven in the back and an open kitchen where you can watch your dough being tossed into the air.

"Are you kidding?" Nero says. "If they tried to close it, people would riot."

He nods to the server and leads me to our old booth in the

back. Same laminated menus, same faded photos on the wall...
I almost feel like we've been transported back in time. Except
we weren't usually—or ever—in formal wear.

"This really takes me back," Nero says, leaning back against
the cracked leather booth.

"You don't come here anymore?" I ask, surprised. The two
of us had decided a long time ago that this was our favorite
pizza of all time. I didn't think he'd stop eating it.

"No."

The word is clipped, and somehow, I know that he hasn't
been back since I left.

But I don't want to go down that road. Not tonight. Nero's
looking about as relaxed as I've seen him so far—at least he was
up until ten seconds ago.

"Hey, do you remember that time a pigeon got in here?" I
ask, changing the subject.

Nero grins, and I realize with a jolt that it's the first
genuine smile I've seen on his face in ten years. It softens his
features in a way that makes my traitorous heart skitter in my
chest.

"How could I forget that? Just strutted in after a customer,
like it was going to order an extra cheese to go."

I laugh. "I don't blame it, I swear I've been dreaming about
this place for years."

We place our order, and soon the waitress arrives at the
table with our pizza, steam coming up off it as she sets it down.
My mouth waters at the smell and when Nero takes a slice to
put on my plate, the cheese stretches in that way that only the
best cheese does.

"Damn," he chuckles. "It's been too long."

It's a little too hot to eat immediately, but my stomach is
growling, so I take a bite, only for sauce to burn me. "Oww!"

"You always were so impatient," Nero smirks.

"I'm impulsive." I correct him, blowing on the slice to cool it.

"Uh huh." Nero grins, devouring his slice in one.

"What, do you have a radioactive mouth or something?" I protest, jealous.

"Pretty much. Surprised I have any tastebuds left, after all the bad tequila Chase and I used to drink." Nero eats another, then sits back, taking a break.

There's laughter from a table nearby and we glance over to see a couple sitting together on one side of a booth, obviously on a date. They kiss, snuggling together.

I feel a pang, and when I glance over at Nero, I see him watching them for a moment longer. When he finally turns back to me, he almost looks regretful.

"Do you ever wonder who you might be, if things had gone differently?"

I blink, surprised by the question, and the raw honesty in his voice.

"Sure I do," I reply quietly. "You think I planned to waitress for a living in some shitty Vegas dive?"

Nero grimaces. "Don't remind me about that. Fuck, you were the last person I expected when I walked through that door."

"That makes the two of us."

We exchange a wry look, acknowledging how weird our situation is. And maybe it's the unexpected memories, or the hit of cheese and carbs, but I pause.

"I always wanted to go to art school," I admit quietly. "You know, it was my big dream to go to Europe after high school and see all the galleries in Paris. Walk the streets and get inspired by the culture. Even if I'd been dead broke, I like to think I would have found a way."

"I remember watching you paint," Nero says quietly. "You

were so talented. You had such a unique way of seeing the world."

Our eyes meet, and I feel a well of emotion rise in my chest. I'm seeing a glimpse of my Nero, the person I knew before everything changed. "Did you keep it up?" he asks.

"The painting?" I shake my head. "It was hard to find the time. And painting... It was always my way of expressing myself. But once we were pretending to be a different family, it seemed... I don't know, like it would be dangerous to be that honest, even on the canvas."

Nero frowns. "I'm sorry," he says. "That your art was taken away from you."

Our gaze grows more intense. I have to look away. "It's fine," I say quickly, and focus on the food again.

"What about you?" I ask. "Do you ever think about a different life?"

He shrugs, his eyes on his plate. "There never been any point in that for me. I was born for this. Raised to be the Barretti boss."

There's a darkness in his expression, but it's not anger. Something more like regret. A world-weary look that makes me wonder.

What kind of crimes are in his past? What kind of things has he seen?

I swallow, trying to block memories of those photos again. But just like always, Nero can see through me.

He clears his throat. "Listen, about what you saw the other day... That guy..."

Oh, God. I can't listen to this. I thought that I wanted to know, but now that he's going to tell me, I don't want details.

"No," I blurt. "You don't have to—"

"I do," he cuts me off. "I want you to know. He was a bad guy, Lily. I know it's hard to believe, but he deserved it."

"Deserved a beating like that?" I respond, silently adding, 'to death.'

Nero gives a grim nod. "He raped a girl."

My jaw drops. Whatever justifications I was expecting, it wasn't this.

"What...?" I stammer, shocked. "What are you talking about?"

"The kid's mom came to us," Nero says, peeling the label off his beer bottle. "Her dad's done some work for me in the past, but he's a drunk now. He couldn't..." he shakes his head. "So, the mom came to me. The girl's fourteen," he adds, fury in his voice. "That bastard picked her up on her way home from the grocery store. Didn't let her go for two days."

Tears prick at my eyes. "Oh my God," I whisper. "Is she...?"

"Alive? Yeah, not that she wants to be," Nero says grimly. "We've got her in a treatment place upstate. Therapists, the whole nine yards. They say she'll come through it in the end, but..." His fists tighten involuntarily. "Shit like that doesn't happen on my watch," he tells me, eyes burning. "It's on me to keep my people safe. And a scumbag like that walking around... He had to pay. I had to take care of it."

"Of course you did," I answer automatically. His head snaps up, like he thinks I'm being sarcastic, but I mean it, every word. I reach across and take his hand without thinking, squeezing it tightly. "Don't even apologize. That guy deserved everything he got."

Nero exhales. "But still... I'm the one who had to do it. Whatever shit goes down... It always falls to me."

He meets my eyes for a long moment, our hands intertwined, and I realize, the Barretti crown isn't just status, or power. It's a responsibility, too. Nero may operate by a fucked up moral code, but it's his to enforce.

My heart aches for him.

"It must be lonely," I whisper. "Having to carry all of that alone."

Nero pulls his hand away. "You don't know anything about my life."

"I didn't mean—" I try to apologize, but the shutters are already slamming down in his eyes, severing our moment of connection.

His jaw tightens and his shoulders get stiff. "It's time to go," he says gruffly, getting to his feet.

"But the pizza..." I say.

He scowls, our intimacy forgotten. "I've had better."

But despite Nero's 180-degree snap back to icy hostility, everything feels different now. He's confided in me—trusted me—and I can't help but see him differently.

Is he really the monster that Agent Greggs makes him out to be? The monster I've been only too happy to believe he is?

I turn it over in my mind all during the ride back to his place, but I come no closer to an answer. All I know is, seeing this glimpse of the conflict brewing behind his steely gaze is chipping away at my defenses.

Defenses I'm relying on to keep my desire at bay.

Inside, Nero shoves the leftover pizza in the refrigerator. I wonder if he still eats it cold for breakfast, but I don't ask.

I know that the time for reliving the past is over. Still, I linger in the hallway, wondering if there's any way to keep our connection alive. "Do you need me for anything tomorrow?" I ask. "For McKenna, I mean." I add, when my voice comes out too eager.

"I'll let you know." Nero's reply is curt.

I bite back my disappointment. "Goodnight then."

He glances over, and his eyes meet mine. I can feel a charged spark in the air, one that curls around my torso and shoots straight to my core.

Heat floods my body. But Nero just clenches his jaw. "Night," he growls, turning away.

I hurry to my room and lock the door behind me. I change for bed, and go through the motions of my skincare routine, but even when I slide under the covers, my body is still wound tight.

Wanting him.

I exhale a frustrated breath. Every time I close my eyes, I'm back in that cabin, pressed up against the wall with Nero's hands pinning me in place; his fingers thrusting high inside me, making me moan.

Making me beg.

My pulse kicks, and I throw the covers back, too hot. Too restless. Too much of everything.

I slide my hands over my body, wishing they were Nero's. I let myself sink into the memory, running my fingertips over my lips as I remember his heated kiss, the way he consumed me, dominated my mouth with his tongue.

My own touch is light as it runs down my neck and chest. I use both hands to cup my breasts, pinching my nipples just enough to turn them into hardened peaks.

Holding onto the image of Nero in my mind, his lust-filled eyes, and the dirty words he spoke into my ear, I slowly slide one hand between my thighs. My touch isn't anywhere close to being as satisfying as his thick, searching fingers, but I begin to circle my clit—needing that pressure, aching for release.

The fantasy in my mind changes, and I picture my door flying open as Nero comes charging in. Determined to finish what we started at the cabin.

Vowing to claim me for real.

I slip two fingers inside of my body as I picture him lining himself up at my entrance and sinking in deep. The thought of him riding me hard and slow makes me moan deep in my throat.

He'd be demanding. Merciless. But not in a selfish way. No, Nero would draw out my pleasure as long as he could, until I can't take anymore.

Until I'm screaming his name, swearing anything under the sun.

Until I'm his again.

My breathing grows labored. I can feel the pleasure building inside of me, so I move back to my clit, stroking swiftly in the rhythm that usually gets me there.

But not tonight.

I'm close, so fucking close, but for some reason, I can't get over the edge. I can't let go.

Fuck.

I let out a scream into the pillow, wound so tight, with release out of reach. This is all Nero's fault. Now that I've had a taste of the kind of pleasure he can give me, nothing else will get me there.

I need him. His fingers. His mouth.

His cock.

Fuck.

I lay there, waiting for the ache to subside, but I'm flooded with frustration, so I get up and throw on a robe, heading through the dark apartment to the kitchen. A pint of ice-cream is about the only satisfaction I'm going to get tonight, so I find a tub of Haagen Dasz from the freezer, and grab a spoon.

But just as I'm digging in, a noise makes me startle. "Hello?" I yelp, whirling around. "Is anyone there?"

"It's my damn apartment." Nero emerges from the shadows, dressed in grey sweatpants and a thin T-shirt. He crosses to the fridge and grabs a bottle of water as I cover my racing heart with my hand and try to catch my breath.

"You scared me."

"Why?" Nero smirks. "You think anyone would be dumb enough to break in here?"

I try to ignore the fact I was just having triple-X rated fantasies about the man standing just a few feet away from me. "I don't know what kind of company you keep."

"Jealous?"

The question hangs in the dim light between us.

I scoff. "Keep dreaming."

"Oh, you don't want to know about my dreams, Princess." Nero catches my hand as I pass, pulling me in close to him.

My breath hitches. His eyes meet mine, amusement in the dark, stormy depths. "Or maybe you do..." He purrs, inhaling slowly.

He lifts my hand to his mouth, and slowly licks my fingers.

The fingers I was using to touch myself.

I gasp, stunned.

"Delicious," he says, his voice low. His gaze turns hungry, roving over my body. "Did you come thinking about me?"

I yank my hand back, shocked. "I don't know what you're talking about," I lie, as my cheeks flush hot.

"Oh, I think you do." Nero follows me back, trapping me against the cool metal of the refrigerator. His body presses closer, his breath is hot on my ear as he leans in, murmuring, "I think you've been rubbing that pretty cunt of yours, whimpering for me to come fill it all the way up."

Desire crashes through me, and I clench, turned on. "How did you know...?" I stutter, reeling.

Nero sees it too in my reaction, and a smile of cruel victory spreads across his face. "I could smell it on you, Princess. You smell like sex."

His teeth nip at my earlobe, and I shudder, my legs going

weak. I was wound tight before I even walked into the kitchen, but now?

Now I'm shaking. It feels like just one touch, and I'll crash over the edge of that climax I was chasing.

The one my own hands couldn't provide.

Nero runs one possessive hand down my body, gauging my unsteady state. "Or maybe you didn't get what you needed, hmmm? Maybe you came out here in this skimpy tank top, looking for me to finish the job." He plucks at one of my stiff nipples, sending a shock of sensation through me.

"I didn't..." I protest weakly, but I know deep down, he's right. It wasn't a late-night snack I was looking for to sate my appetite.

It was *him*.

"Yeah, you need it bad, don't you, baby?" Nero presses *right there* between my legs, and fuck, even through the cotton of my pajama pants, it's enough to make me cry out in pleasure. "My perfect princess is all wound up, wet and needy to take my cock."

He rubs my clit slowly, and I whimper, too far gone to try pretending anymore. "Yes," I gasp, bucking against his fingers. "Please, I need..."

"What do you need?" Nero demands.

I bite back a sob. "You. I need you inside me. I want your cock."

There's silence for a moment, and then Nero steps back. Cool air hits my body where his hot muscle was just covering me and for a terrible moment, I think he's going to leave me like this. Turn me on, and walk away, laughing at my aching need.

But what he says next is so much better. And so much worse.

"You want it? You'll get it, baby." Nero shoves down his sweatpants and frees himself, fisting the thick, gorgeous length of his cock in his hand. "But you've got to earn the privilege of riding this beast. Get on your knees and open that pretty mouth."

Holy shit!

Lust brings me to my knees without hesitation, eager to do as he says. Anything to stay in this wild haze of desire, sex beating through my body like a drum.

Nero lets out a low curse, looking down at me. "Fuck, Princess, look at you..."

But I'm looking at him, every thick, straining inch of his cock. Dear God, he's massive. My heart is pounding in my chest as he reaches out and cradles the back of my head, guiding me forwards. But I don't need the instruction. I lean in, hungrily wrapping my hands around the base of his cock and licking up along the thick shaft in one long swoop.

Nero groans. Power slips through me, mingling with my own lust in an intoxicating blend. I lick him again, teasing over the stiff length of him and swirling my tongue lightly over the head. I revel in the taste of him, clean and masculine, so big, I don't know if I can take him all.

But fuck, I'm going to have fun trying.

I pump gently with my hand as I lick over him again, exploring every stiff, velvet inch, until Nero's grip on my hair tightens. "Enough teasing," he growls. "It's time to open wide and suck."

He thrusts towards my face, and I do as he says: I hollow out my cheeks and take him deep inside my mouth.

Damn. The feeling is incredible. Nero's hands are in my hair, controlling my motions as he pulls me off him all the way to the tip, then thrusts deep again, bringing me back. Fucking my mouth. It's a harsh, wild rhythm, and I can feel his body tense; hear his labored breath and the ragged groans of pleasure spilling from his mouth.

"Fuck, baby, just like that. Yeah, every last inch. Oh *fuck*."

His words make me even hotter. I pump him harder with my hand as I take him even deeper. It stings a little, and I have to blink back the tears that automatically smart in my eyes, but I don't stop. I don't want to stop. The world has contracted to just this moment, the feel of his grip and the wild thrust of his hips, and the thick, meaty length of his cock pistoning between my lips.

I blindly reach my free hand between my thighs as I moan around him, rubbing at my clit in a swift, jerky pace. God, I'm close again, so close, as Nero pumps between my lips, his words growing more desperate, his own climax within reach.

Because of me.

"That's right, baby, don't stop," he groans, pumping harder, so deep I almost gag. "It's so good. Fuck, *fuck*, just like that."

I feel my own body clench, ready for release too. Power sings in my veins. For the first time, I'm the one in control of *his* pleasure. I'm the one making him beg.

My tongue swirls and I go faster and faster, relaxing my jaw as much as possible. I know that he's close, his hips bucking, out of control. I pull back, almost to the tip, and then angle my head, taking him all the way to the back of my throat.

"Fuck!" Nero roars. His body jerks, and then he's coming, ribbons of hot climax spurting down my throat as he holds on tight to me, surging into my mouth. "Swallow it, baby," he groans, thrusting again, again. "Drink up what your man is giving you. Every last drop."

I obey without thinking, and God, the feeling of his release is enough to send me hurtling over the precipice of my own orgasm. Pleasure shatters through me, and I shudder, so overwhelmed with sex and power I feel dizzy. Drunk on the moment.

Intoxicated by *him*.

Nero inhales a ragged breath, finally releasing me. He steps back, eyes raking over me... And coming to rest on the hand I still have nestled between my legs. His lips curl in a smile.

"Couldn't wait, could you?"

I sit back on my heels, gasping for breath. I feel incredible. I feel invincible.

Then the sound of a cellphone comes, somewhere in the loft. The spell is broken. Nero looks up, distracted. It's late now, and we both know, a call like that can't be good news.

Not in his line of work.

"Go," I say instinctively. I can sense the switch is coming—when he remembers that he resents me, and all our tangled history—and I want to preempt it. I don't want to taint what just happened here. And how much I loved it.

When I see the relief flash in his eyes, I know I made the right call.

"Goodnight," he tells me softly, then he turns to go.

I watch him disappear down the hallway, and close his office door, leaving me gasping on my knees, after the most intense sexual experience of my life.

And already, I want more.

17

LILY

I WAKE up the next morning to an empty apartment. It's something of a relief to realize that Nero has left. I need the time to clear my head after everything that's happened, and I know that's impossible when he's near.

Getting into the shower, I take my time cleaning my body, enjoying the feeling of the hot water cascading over me. Memories flood back in my mind, the feeling of his hands in my hair... His groaned filthy words... *His cock in my mouth.*

God, it was so good, even the feeling of running the loofa over my breasts makes my nipples form hard peaks and there's a pulsing in my sensitive core. He's driving me crazy, and he's not even in the building. All I want is for him to come back, set me against the wall and—

Nope. Down, girl.

I put the shower head back and step out of the shower before I can get lost in the haze of desire.

I need to think clearly.

My position is so precarious, being swept up by my hormones is not an option. Not when so much on the line.

Getting tangled up with Nero sexually is just about the dumbest thing I could do, given everything else that's going on, but my body just won't listen to sense.

I dry off and dress for the day, casual in linen pants and a cute shirt. Catching sight of my reflection in the mirror, though, it's clear from my flushed cheeks and swollen lips, I've only got one thing on my mind.

Dammit. I feel like I'm caught in a war between reason and desire. Logically, I know I need to be playing the angles, figuring how to get this McKenna deal done and get out, but that's hard to do when I'm with Nero. All the tension between us takes on a life of its own, like gravity is pulling us together.

Blotting out the past—and the uncertainties of my future.

I see glimpses of goodness in him, that's what makes this so hard. Flashes of tenderness. That possessive concern that makes my toes curl. He's got the world on his shoulders, and a part of me wants to be the one to make that all disappear, at least for a little while. On my knees last night, seeing the fierce desire in his gaze, knowing I was the only thing that mattered in the world to him in that moment...

That's the sex talking, Lily. Not common sense.

I snap out of it. Sitting around this loft all day reliving our sexy encounters isn't going to help me get a grip on the situation. With everything else spinning out of control, I need to feel centered, more like myself again.

And I suddenly get an idea of how I can make it happen.

"WELCOME TO ROTH ART SUPPLY," a clerk calls over, as I walk in the door. "Can I help you find anything in particular?"

I look around at the huge space, aisles packed with paint

and canvases, and a million other things besides. I begin to smile. "I'm just browsing for now," I tell her.

"If you need anything, give me a yell."

I take a deep breath, and wander down the first aisle, already feeling a hundred percent better. It's been too long since I did this. I've barely picked up a paintbrush in years, but right now, it's exactly the distraction I need.

I browse for over an hour, loving every minute of it. I load up on various sizes of canvases, paints, brushes, and anything else I could possibly need. I even buy a stool to sit on. It's the ultimate shopping spree, and the best part is, I don't even look at prices as I shop. It's funny, I must have charged Nero's credit card a hundred times this amount by now on designer clothing and accessories for all his fancy events, but this is the first time I've felt almost giddy over the freedom of his unlimited budget.

Finally, I call it a day, and leave the store, arranging to have everything delivered to the loft. When I get back, I take a tour of the apartment with new eyes, looking for the perfect space to turn into my new art studio.

If I'm going to be cooped up in this place for much longer, I may as well start feeling at home.

There are a couple of unused rooms, but when I step into a sunny den at the back of the loft, I know I've found the one. The ten-foot-tall windows bring in amazing light, and it has an airy feel that transports me away from the city. I shove the couch to the side of the wall and move some of the stuff to the closet.

There are a couple of battered boxes shoved in the back, and I pause, curious. Everything else in this apartment is so impersonal, but inside, I find a hoard of Nero's old childhood keepsakes.

I pick through them, feeling a pang of recognition. A little trophy from when Nero's Little League team won the series championship one year, pictures of him as a boy and teenager, a Transformers toy. They are small things that would only have been held onto if they held some sort of sentimental significance. I'm both surprised that he's held onto stuff like this, and simultaneously not at all surprised that it's all been packed away and left seemingly without another thought.

I want to look through all of it, to explore what he deemed worth holding onto, but I'm worried that it will just make me feel more connected to him, reminding me of the boy I used to know. I can't keep looking at him through the man through rose-colored glasses. It's messing with my emotions.

It might be hard to reconcile Nero's past and present, but at least I know who I am. Once the art purchases are delivered, I don't waste any time getting them set up in my new studio. I position the easel in front of the window, turn on some upbeat music, and lay out my new supplies.

I feel like a kid on Christmas morning, unwrapping all my goodies. Smiling, I decide to play with the oil paints first. As I start prepping the canvas, I can feel something inside of me change. I'm relaxed, everything feels simple again.

I feel like myself for the first time in ages.

Standing in front of the easel, I start sketching lightly with some pencils, starting a base for an image that suddenly pops into my mind.

It's a charming bistro on a street corner in Paris, the kind of place with a red awning and plenty of outdoor seating. There are cars on the street and a couple walking down the sidewalk, their bodies close together and their hands touching. In love.

I stand back, surprised by the picture taking shape in front of me. I don't know where it came from, maybe my conversation with Nero the other night about living a different life. It isn't just a 'what if?' to me, but a comfort, too. I must have daydreamed about Paris a thousand times those first years we were stuck in Witness Protection. I'd close my eyes at night and try to imagine myself a thousand miles away from the small, cheap apartment, and my parents' fighting, and all the half-truths I had to tell to make it through the day unnoticed. I'd fantasize about Nero showing up on my doorstep, whisking us off, having the life I always dreamed of.

But soon enough, I knew I had to let the dream die. Nobody was going to whisk me anywhere. And thinking about those 'what-ifs' caused me more pain than comfort.

But now…?

Now, I feel my imagination return, losing myself in my work as I lay down the first base colors, building the details and light in the scene.

I'm not sure how long I've been working when I pause to sip some water. I hear a sound behind me. It's small, just the brushing of fabric that comes from someone putting their hands in their pockets maybe. Or shrugging off a jacket.

It's not meant to get my attention.

But I turn anyway and find Nero standing just inside the open door. He's watching me, leaning against the doorframe, taking in the sight of my painting.

"Hi," I blurt, off-guard. "I didn't hear you get in. How long have you been there?"

"Not long," he says. "I didn't want to interrupt."

I blush, suddenly self-conscious of the mess I've made in his home. "Sorry, I probably should have asked before taking over the room," I say, starting to clean up. "But I just got all this stuff, and couldn't wait to get started."

"It's fine," he says. His eyes go to the painting again, and he looks as if he's about to say something more. Then he stops.

"I got word about the real estate zoning meeting today," he says again, his tone shifting. "It's been set for next week. We're running out of time to get McKenna on board."

I gulp. Running out of time for his deal... and my future safety.

"Is there another event we can go to?" I ask. "Something that would give us a chance to get close to McKenna, play the game a little."

"Maybe. I'm checking his schedule. But for now..." Nero pauses, and clears his throat. "Would you have dinner with me?"

I stop dead in shock at the question.

"I..." I blink, thrown. Is he asking me out on a date? He hasn't voluntarily spent time alone with me since I was brought here. And he definitely hasn't asked. He's summoned, or dragged, or ordered me. Never an invitation.

I search his expression, but it's unreadable.

"I... OK," I finally reply. "Just as long as it's not my last meal!"

Nero doesn't blink at my quip. "Be ready to leave in an hour. I have business to attend to, but I'll meet you there."

He leaves, and a moment later, I hear the main door shut behind him. I turn back to the canvas, still reeling. But whatever work was in progress, there's no way I can focus now, not with a potential date looming in just an hour.

Is this for real?

I quickly clean my brushes and wash up, before heading to my room and turning my focus to something entirely different: what to wear.

I don't know where we're going, and when it comes to Nero, nothing is off the table. I think about our old pizza spot. I reach for a casual pair of jeans, then pause. What if we end up at a fancy restaurant or something?

And why do I care so much?

I tell myself, this isn't anticipation, but wariness. Who knows what Nero has in store?

Going with my gut, I rifle through my closet until I come across the one thing every woman should own, a little black dress. It's simple but sexy, and it could technically fit in almost anywhere.

Yes, this is the best option.

That decision made, I should be able to get ready quickly, but I find myself lingering over simple things, like how to wear my hair and which pair of heels look best. It's all because I'm nervous, not that I would ever admit that to Nero. I don't like this feeling of uncertainty that I have about what's really happening between us. I can think of the sexual encounters as a game, an erotic thrill, but there's no denying that the dynamic between us is changing.

Is this becoming more than just revenge? More than arranging a real estate deal?

Do I want it to be more?

I'm playing with fire, I know. Because we've been stumbling closer to the edge, but it's still not too late to back off. But if we have sex, if we cross that line...

There'll be no going back.

BY SEVEN, I'm ready to go, so I grab a cute leather jacket, and head down to the lobby. I'm expecting Kyle to meet me inside like usual, but the black G-wagon is idling on the curb outside.

I guess I've upgraded to not needing an escort every time I leave the loft.

I head out, and open the back door, sliding inside. "Evening, Kyle," I say, expecting his usual monotone grunt. When the car doesn't pull away from the curb immediately, I look up.

It's not Kyle behind the wheel.

Instead, I see Chase there, eyes on me in the rearview mirror.

"Chase?" My prickles with anxiety. "What are you doing here?" I remember his rough treatment on the way to New York, and I don't want to be alone with him.

"What does it look like, *Princess*?" His voice twists, ugly, on Nero's familiar nickname. "I'm taking you for a drive. Because it's high time you and I had a little talk."

I hear the unmistakable sound of the car locks clicking into place.

I'm trapped.

18

LILY

I'M IN TROUBLE.

I swallow hard, watching the dark city blur past outside the windows. My heart is beating rapidly with nerves, and all I can do is wonder, is it all over for me?

What does Chase know?

He's a dangerous guy, I know that. He has to be in order to be Nero's right-hand man. I'm terrified of what's coming now, but I can't let it show. A man like this gets off on instilling fear. And probably inflicting pain.

Yep, *real* trouble.

I run through my limited options in my head. I have my cell phone, but what good does that do me? There's no one to call for help. For all I know, Nero has arranged this whole trip.

But why?

Does Nero know that I've been talking to the FBI? I feel a fresh shiver of fear. I haven't said anything to them, but that doesn't matter. If he knew that I was even *meeting* with Agent Greggs, he'd assume the worst.

"Where are we going?" I ask, making myself relax back into

the seat so that I appear unconcerned. I subtly unclick my seat-belt just in case I somehow get an opportunity to run when the car stops. It's not likely, but a girl can dream. "If you wanted to chat, we could have just done it at Nero's place, you know. No need for the dramatics."

"Quiet," he snaps, with a scowl in the rearview mirror. "You'll know soon enough."

He takes a sharp turn, and I have to hang on. I look outside, my fear growing. We've left the buzz of the city behind, and we're bumping along an unpaved track by the river, with run-down warehouses all around. There's nobody around here; the place is deserted.

Nobody to hear a scream. Or a gunshot.

Or worse.

Chase pulls into the parking lot of one of the warehouses. We're the only car here, and the single light coming from above the rusty metal door of the building falls across the lot, giving everything an eerie yellow glow now that it's fully dark out.

He circles around and opens my door. "Get out."

I hesitate. I could try to run, but Chase is fit and maybe even armed. I wouldn't get far, especially not in these heels...

Listing the reasons that I couldn't get away to myself isn't doing me any good, so I get out, and follow him inside the warehouse, as he looks warily around, making sure nobody's in sight.

Inside, the space is empty, with a few shipping containers stacked at one end. There's a couple of bare industrial lights shining brightly on the stained concrete floors – stained with what, I don't want to know.

I flinch at the sound of the door rattling shut behind us. Now I can't keep back the terror that's blooming, icy in my chest.

But I have to. I have to stay calm enough to figure this out.

So, taking a deep breath, I cross my arms in front of my chest and glare at him.

"Ready to talk?" I ask, proud of myself when I manage to sound bored and annoyed instead of terrified. "I have to say, your choice of a rendezvous spot leads something to be desired. I'm guessing there won't be snacks."

"Drop the attitude, Princess," Chase scowls, stepping way too close to me. "This isn't a fucking tea party." He looms over me, broad muscle but with none of Nero's natural grace. Chase is a blunt object, and the look in his eyes is burning resentment.

I force myself to stand tall. "Clearly," I reply. "So why don't you get to the point and save us both this delightful small talk."

His eyes narrow, and I feel another shot of fear. *Maybe I shouldn't be baiting him.*

"I'm on to you." Chase says with a dangerous grin, and my stomach drops.

Fuck!

I panic. He knows about the Feds, about my secret meetings. It's over. In a second, my life flashes before my eyes, all the dreams I'll never get to see come true, and Teddy—

Teddy!

"So, we're going to have that talk now," Chase continues, looking pleased that I'm finally showing fear. "And you're going to tell me everything."

I inhale a shaky breath, freaking the fuck out. What do I do now? Chase isn't like Nero, I won't be able to bargain or beg him for mercy, and if I don't find the right thing to say in the next ten seconds—

Wait a minute.

I stop my panicked thoughts in their tracks, looking around again, realizing something.

Nero isn't here.

"Is Nero coming soon?" I ask, keeping my voice steady. "I

prefer to talk to the boss, you see. Instead of wasting my time with the hired help."

Chase scowls. "I take care of whatever needs to be handled. He doesn't always have to order me around."

There's something about the way that Chase says those words that ignites a glimmer of hope inside of me. Nero didn't arrange this.

But that doesn't make any sense. If this was the end, if they did know about the Feds, there's no way he would miss it. He would be the one standing in front of me, demanding the truth.

"So, you're going rogue?" I ask, I ask, tilting my head as if I felt nothing more than curious. Good thing my arms are crossed, it hides my shaking hands. "That's a big move. He might not be so happy to hear about this."

"Shut up," Chase snaps again, and I can see that I'm getting to him. "Nero trusts *me*. He always has done."

"Uh huh. With... What, exactly?" I ask, my confidence growing. "You still haven't said why I'm here. What it is you're 'on to,' exactly—besides unflattering bootcut jeans."

Chase lunges closer, grabbing my arm, and fear flares again. "I don't know what fucking game you're playing," he growls, squeezing painfully. "But I don't buy this innocent act. You're a traitor, just like your fucking father, and I'm going to get you."

His words sink in. Chase doesn't have anything on me. Not yet.

Relief crashes through me, so hard I almost collapse. It takes everything I have to stay standing and to roll my eyes like the bored princess I'm pretending to be.

"Careful, Chase," I reply. "You know Nero doesn't like people touching what's his."

I look pointedly at his grip on my arm. He releases me, cursing.

"Nero might be cunt struck, but I'm not fooled." His eyes burn into mine. "I'll get you in the end."

I catch my breath. "Right now, you need to get me to my dinner date," I say, haughty. "Or I could call Nero right now, and explain why I'm running late..."

Chase backs up. "I'm watching you," he warns, striding to the door. I have no choice but to follow, and get back into the car, trying to ignore his gaze in the rearview mirror.

That was a close one.

Even though I managed to talk my way out of it, I'm still shaken. I've been so busy worrying about Nero and the FBI that I didn't even realize I needed to worry about Chase. I have enemies on every side.

And the walls are closing in.

IT TURNS out that we're near the docks, which was our destination all along. As Chase pulls up to a parking spot, I see Nero waiting for me. He looks damn good in a black suit, clean-shaven, with his hair still damp from the shower. Behind him, there's a yacht moored at a jetty. I feel my jaw drop as I look at the thing. White with sleek lines, it's luxurious in a way that definitely answers my question about whether this is a date.

If Chase had brought me straight here, I might be swept up in romance, but my mood is too dark now. I slowly get out of the car and approach him.

"Hi," Nero gives a guarded smile as I approach him. Now that I'm closer, I see a candlelit dinner set up on the deck of the yacht behind him.

"Oh." I pause, surprised.

"You like it?" he asks, lips slowly spreading in a smile.

I don't reply. I want to be impressed, and excited, but all I can think about is this perilous tightrope I'm walking. Nothing has changed about my situation—if anything, it's getting more dangerous by the day. My fortunes can change on a dime. I can't afford to let my guard down, even for a moment.

Even with him.

"I figured, it could be nice to get out, away from the apartment for a while," he continues, leading me onboard. "Are you hungry?"

My stomach is rolling from my anxiety, but I nod anyway. "Always!" I lie.

The corner of Nero's mouth ticks up in a grin. "Let me guess, you snacked on the ride over."

"Ha. Yeah. You got me," I lie, feeling out of place and awkward. Whatever it is that he's planned, it's all wrong for the way I'm feeling right now.

We settle at the table. It's a lovely scene, bobbing gently on the evening tide with the lights of the city reflecting off the dark water. There's candles and silverware, and a bottle of champagne chilling in a bucket of ice. Even roses arranged in a crystal vase. The picture of romance.

But all I can think, is *what is he playing at?*

Is this a genuine gesture, or another twisted game? Nero always has an agenda, and whisking me off for a night of romance after all the tension we've been through? It doesn't add up.

What if Chase was lying, and the two of them are working together? Some way to make me drop my defenses and be lulled into trusting him?

I don't know what to believe any more. All I know is that romance is the last thing on my mind.

I pull the white napkin in my lap. Nero lifts the cover off one of the dishes, revealing a delicious looking pasta. There are vegetables, bread, oil...

"I thought we could eat, then head out on the water for a

little cruise," Nero says, pouring champagne. He passes me a glass. "It's pretty cool, seeing the city from this angle."

I give a little nod. "Fine."

I nervously sip my champagne, looking at him across the table. The candlelight softens his features, dark eyes warm on me, but even though I feel that familiar rush of attraction, I know, I can't let myself forget what he's capable of.

I can never forget.

He gulps his champagne. "I don't know if you remember, but this is the same kind we had at that New Year's Eve party."

I do remember. It was just a few months before I left the city. It was the last party we ever had at my house, a big New Year's blowout with just about everyone we knew, including Roman and Nero. My dad wasn't lenient enough to let his sixteen-year-old daughter drink, but it was easy for Nero to grab an extra glass and for the two of us to slip away from the gathering to spend some time alone. He'd taken me to my room, sliding his hand up my dress and bringing me to orgasm for the first time with his fingers.

Before that, I'd only known my own touch, but Nero had a way of working my body into a frenzy that quickly became addicting. That night was the beginning of my entire sex life and just the taste of the champagne on my tongue brings all those memories back to the surface.

I want to lose myself in the past, but I've been doing that far too much lately. My present reality is far too different.

Too dangerous.

I put the glass down, and I pick up my fork. I move the food around on my plate, but I don't eat anything.

Nero eyes me, but he doesn't say anything.

The silence stretches.

"How was your day?" he asks, sounding gruff.

"You know," I reply, confused. "I told you, back at the loft. My painting..."

"Right." Nero clears his throat.

Another pause, and I can't take it anymore. I don't know what he's thinking, playing at romance and dating when our situation is so fucked up, but I don't want to spend another hour pretending this is all fine, and we don't share a decade of twisted history.

I push my plate away. "I'm sorry, but I have the worst headache," I lie, with an apologetic smile. "It must have been all the paint fumes."

Nero's brow furrows. "I can send someone to the drugstore for painkillers," he suggests, but I shake my head.

"I think I just need to go lie down. Have an early night. Can we go?"

His jaw tightens, but he gives a nod. "Of course."

WE DRIVE BACK to the loft in silence. I sneak glances over at Nero, but he's scrolling on his phone, looking tense. I sigh. I don't even know what he was trying to do with that whole romantic dinner scene, but now it's over, I'm still just as confused. One minute, he's making it clear he can't wait to be rid of me, the next, he's setting up a thoughtful dinner. And my own emotions are just as confusing: I must ricochet between loathing and lust a hundred times a day.

And when he touches me... None of that even matters anymore.

Arriving at his building, we head upstairs to the loft. "Well..." I say, awkward, just inside the doorway. "I should get to bed."

"Wait," Nero orders me. I watch him stride to the guest bathroom, and rummage in the cabinet. He brings me a pack of

Ibuprofen. "For your head," he says, eyes searching my face like he doesn't believe my flimsy excuse.

I smile weakly. "Thanks. I'm sure I'll be fine."

I start to go to my room, but his voice stops me. "You don't have to lie. You can just say you don't want to be alone with me."

I turn back. "What?" I ask, confused.

Nero gives a tense shrug, avoiding my eyes. "I wanted to do something nice for you. After... all of *this*."

My jaw drops, and I feel a treacherous flush of emotion. Softening me.

He was trying to make me happy.

But then Nero pulls himself together. "But clearly, you couldn't wait to get away from me. Or maybe the evening wasn't up to your high standards," he adds, voice twisting sarcastically. "Yacht not big enough for you, *Princess*?"

I shake my head. The dinner was genuine, I realize. But now he's angry I didn't go along with the romantic make-believe? "I can't believe this!" I exclaim, anger rising. "After everything I've been through tonight, you're mad that I wasn't in the mood to sip champagne and stare at the stars?"

"What are you talking about?" Nero asks.

It's just like I suspected. He didn't know about Chase's attempt to intimidate me.

"Your evil henchman decided to take a little detour before dinner," I explain bitterly. "Chase took me out to some deserted warehouse in the middle of nowhere. It didn't exactly put me in the mood."

Nero's face changes. "Did he hurt you?" he demands, stepping forward.

"No, but he scared me half to death, threatening to have me killed!" I reply. "Going on about how I'm keeping secrets, and he's going to find me out. Tell him to back the hell off, OK?"

"Maybe he has good reason not to trust you." Nero narrows his eyes. "What *have* you been playing at?"

"Trying to help you land this deal with McKenna!" I cry, ignoring my guilty pang. Lying isn't just a choice here. It's a necessity. "I've been busting my ass trying to land you this stupid zoning vote, and this is the thanks I get?"

Nero's expression turns dangerous. "I show my appreciation by letting you live."

"I guess that makes you a fucking hero," I retort. "You know what? You *and* Chase can go straight to hell."

I storm to my room and slam the door, but it doesn't make me feel any better. I sink down on the bed, staring at the bottle in my hand. If only I could just take a pill and make all of this better, but it's not a simple headache I'm dealing with here. My web of lies is growing more tangled.

One day soon, a thread is going to snap.

19

NERO

I DON'T SLEEP.

It's not just sexual frustration keeping me up all night, although God knows I have plenty of that. It's the damn fight we had. I don't want to admit to myself that Lily's gotten under my skin, but the evidence is clear.

I planned a fucking candlelight dinner. I rented a yacht.

I picked out a thousand-dollar bottle of champagne, for Christ's sake.

What the hell are you playing at?

I ask myself the question over and over, but I don't have a good answer. Truth is, I don't know what I was thinking, but there was something about seeing her in front of that canvas, lost in her painting, that made me want more of that for her.

More normalcy. More good times. More of the things she deserves.

I thought maybe for one night, we could put all the fucked-up bullshit aside, and just be *us* again. The way things used to be.

I should have known that those days were over the minute her family betrayed the Barretti name.

The minute Lily lied to my face, and pretended she loved me, when all the while, she knew exactly what her father was doing.

Fuck.

I drag myself out of bed the next morning, cursing the day I walked into that Vegas strip club. It would all be so much easier if I'd never laid eyes on her again. Or even turned a blind eye— just walked on back to a private room, and let Lily live out her life far away from me and my dark, violent world.

Then, maybe things would be simple. Maybe I wouldn't be risking everything at the chance to keep her alive, feeling things I have no business feeling.

Emotions that could leave me for dead or bring the destruction of the Barretti empire, an empire that I've sacrificed my whole life to build.

I HEAD over to the club, to get caught up on business. My office there is a damn sanctuary compared to the loft, there's no risk of Lily waltzing through in her yoga pants, ready to get me hard as a rock. But even though I try to distract myself with paperwork, I'm still wound too tight, ready to blow.

And when Chase strolls in like nothing's happened, it's the perfect storm.

"I'm busy," I growl.

"Who pissed in your Cheerios?" Chase asks, looking completely unconcerned. He dumps a bag of bagels on my desk and makes himself comfortable.

"You want to tell me what the fuck you're playing at?" I shoot back, my voice like stone. "What the hell did you do with Lily last night?"

Chase scoffs, rolling his eyes. "What'd she say?"

I frown. Why isn't he answering me directly?

"She said that you threatened her."

"So what if I did?" Chase shrugs. "I'm only looking out for you, man. That bitch can't be trusted."

I glare back. "I'll be the judge of that."

"Yeah? Well, your good judgement isn't working so well these days, not with your dick leading the way," he replies. "C'mon, I thought you'd see through her little Miss Innocent act by now. That woman has an agenda."

I shift, uneasy. "She knows the deal. McKenna for her life."

"And what if someone offers her a better deal?" Chase demands. His good humor slips, and I can see the resentment burning in her eye. "What the fuck are you thinking? If you want a tight piece of ass, go get it, nothing's stopping you. But keeping her close? Running around all those fancy parties? The guys are talking," he adds.

"Saying what?" I ask, controlling my temper.

"That you're losing sight of what really matters. The business. The *family*," he stresses. "All this real estate, pie-in-the-sky bullshit, when we don't need the liability. The machine works, we already run this city—the part that counts. You don't need to fuck up what ain't broke."

I meet his eyes, warning. "Are the guys saying that?" I ask, my voice like ice. "Or you?"

Chase seems to realize his mistake. We might be friends, but I'm still the boss around here.

"Hey, I just thought you should know," he says, holding his hands up. "I've got your back, but that bitch... She's getting to be a problem."

"That bitch is the key to taking this whole organization legit," I ground out. "We close this deal, and it's a whole new ballgame. No more turf wars leaving bodies in the street. No more bullshit from the Feds, or guys risking their necks every time they go to meet a shipment. You want to talk to me about this organization?" I add, getting to my feet. "About family? Everything I do is for that reason. Everything."

Chase looks away. "Yeah, well... I don't trust her, is all."

"It's not your place to question my priorities. You do what I tell you, and that means leaving Lily the fuck alone, unless I tell you otherwise."

"Yes, *boss*."

Chase leaves without another word, and I sit back, thinking about what he just said. Not the part about Lily, because hell if I know whether I can trust her either, but about the rumors swirling.

Because as much as I hate to admit it, he's got a point. My place at the top of this empire depends on two things: Fear, and reward. I've been so focused on securing the kind of cash that would make our dirty dealings pale in comparison that I've neglected the other part of my role. To rule the Barretti activities with an iron fist, so that nobody even thinks about fucking with us. Rival gangs, local cops, officials, business partners, my own damn crew... The list goes on.

If any one of them questions me, or senses any weakness...

They won't hesitate to stab me in the back—or put a bullet in my head. My name may have gotten me the crown when my father went to jail, but it hasn't kept me on the throne this long. No, that's all my own doing.

Which means one wrong move on my part can bring about my *undoing*, too.

"You look like hell."

I look up. Avery's in the doorway, dressed casual as usual in dark jeans and heavy boots, with a fuck-you smirk on her face. "It's one of those days," I sigh, relieved to find a friendly face and not more guys looking to pick a fight. "What's up?"

"You said you had some paperwork for me to sign?"

"Oh. Right."

I gesture her in and find the file. "Renewal on the liquor license here, and that new place we're opening on tenth avenue."

"Another spot in my booming nightlife empire?" Avery asks, teasing. "Lucky me. I'll be on the Forbes list soon at this rate."

She sits and doesn't even glance the documents before signing at the tabbed pages. It's all just a front. Sure, the bars make decent money, but they're also cash businesses: The perfect way to launder our not-so-clean money and have it come out sparkling new.

"Done and done." Avery slides the pages back to me. "Does this mean I'm getting a raise?"

I snort. "Don't push it."

I file the papers away carefully. I learned from my dad's imprisonment just how important it was to keep accurate financial records for those businesses. That was how the FBI ended up getting him behind bars in the end. Just like Al Capone. Tax evasion—and testimony about all his dodgy financial dealings, courtesy of Lily's father.

So, after Roman got sent away, I overhauled. everything. New lawyers, new accountants—ones I could trust. And new names for the liquor board, too. Technically, Avery owns the clubs and bars that really belong to the organization—thanks to her squeaky clean record. Back in the day, her mom did the same for Roman.

"Look at us," Avery says with a smirk, going to pour us a couple of glasses of whisky from my bar in the corner. "Following in our parents' footsteps."

"They'd be so proud," I agree dryly, taking a glass.

"What's the word from old Roman?" she asks, sitting down

and kicking her boots up on the corner of my desk. "You been by to see him yet this month?"

I shake my head. "Busy," I reply shortly.

Avery gives me a look. "I bet he wouldn't be thrilled to head there's a Fordham hanging around... Still breathing."

I sigh. That's exactly the damn reason I haven't gone to pay my usual respects.

Because I know exactly what my father would say about Lily.

And it would be an execution order.

Not to mention, if he found out the reason that I've been keeping her around, this whole real estate deal...

"Do you think I'm being an idiot?" I ask Avery. I've known her long enough to know, she'll give it to me straight.

She sips her drink. "About what? You'll need to narrow it down."

"Ha ha," I roll my eyes. "About Lily."

Avery pauses. "That depends... Not if she's just a tool to get you what you want."

I swirl whiskey around my glass. "And if she's not? If it's more complicated than that?"

Avery's smile turns rueful. "It always is."

I wonder, not for the first time, what Avery has going on that I don't know about. She plays her cards close to her chest about her own love life, but I get the sense there's something going on. "That's not an answer."

"It's the best I've got." She gets up and drains her glass. "But whatever it is between the two of you, it better be worth the risk."

AVERY'S WORDS stay with me as I finish up business and finally head home. It's late, and I'm hoping Lily will have turned in by the time I get back, but no such luck. The lights are on, and I can hear music coming from her new makeshift art studio.

I follow the sound down the hall, to the open doorway. I know I should continue, and head straight to bed to drink myself into unconsciousness, but I can't help pausing to look.

Lily's painting, barefoot in a loose summer dress, her golden hair spilling out of a braid like silk.

Fuck.

She's still the most beautiful thing I've ever seen, and watching her like this, so absorbed in her work...

Every part of me craves to claim her. *Own her.* Give her everything she's been wanting—and more.

Because I know she wants it too. It's there in the way her body sways against me, the breathy way she moans when I kiss her.

The wildfire in her eyes last night, when she fell to her knees and sucked me off like her mouth was made to pleasure me.

Fuck it.

Determination takes root—and frustration, too. I've been holding back since the day I saw her again, keeping her at arm's length in case she finds a way beneath my defenses. Allowing myself only a brief taste of her sweetness, her passion. But all that's done is wind me tighter. Made me need her more.

She's like oxygen, and I'm starving for a single breath.

This isn't me. She's running rings around me, making me less of a man with every minute that passes. Every second I'm not buried to the hilt in her slick cunt, taking what's mine.

What's always been mine.

I step into the room. Lily turns. "What are you—" she starts to ask, but then her voice fades.

She can see it in my eyes, how much I want her. And damn,

if the flare of desire I see there doesn't make my blood hot and my cock hard.

She wants me too.

"Enough with the games," I tell her in a growl, moving forwards. Ready to show her exactly what kind of man I've become. The ways I can make her scream.

I'm Nero fucking Barretti, and I'm done waiting.

"Take off your clothes."

20

LILY

I STARE AT NERO, my heart in my throat.

"You heard me, Princess." His voice drops as he closes the distance between us, low and seductive, like molasses dripping down my spine. "Take off your clothes."

"I..." I gasp for air, lust drowning me in an instant. "I don't know..."

"Yeah, you do." Nero reaches me, taking the brush from my hand and setting it down before cupping my cheek possessively. "You know exactly what's going to happen now, because you've been wet for me since the day we met."

My mouth drops open in shock, but he just chuckles. "And don't try pretending you don't like it when I talk dirty to you, either." he leans in closer, his breath hot on my ear. "We both know, nothing makes that pussy tighter than hearing all the ways I'm going to stretch it out."

Oh my god.

I swear, my legs go weak, and a rush of heat spirals straight to my core.

"It's OK, baby," Nero holds me up, pressing me against his

body. The hard length of him. And fuck, if that doesn't send my system haywire all over again. "I've got you now. And I'm going to show you everything you've been missing all these years," he vows, eyes dark on mine. "Every last inch."

His mouth claims me. There's no other way to put it, the way he kisses me like he's marking his territory, branding me inside and out.

And I love it, every moment.

I can't deny it any longer. Everything he's saying is true. I want him past reason, past any care to my safety or future. All of it is blotted out by the force of his animal magnetism and this wild chemistry, pulling me into his arms and drawing my arms up around his neck before I can even form a single thought. A word.

A reason why not to surrender to the maddening desire crashing through every part of me.

His kiss is rough, and I can feel the hard ridge of his erection pressing into my center, making me moan into his mouth. God, it's so good already, and we've barely begun. I felt strung tight with need as Nero traced the seam of my lips with his tongue. I didn't hesitate to open for him, allowing his tongue to slip inside and tangle with my own. It's a sweet relief as I give in to him.

"Fuck, Lily..." Nero groans, nipping at my lower lip, kneading his hands over my ass. "Do you know how crazy you've been making me?"

"Not as crazy as you make me," I reply breathlessly. So crazy, I climb the man. I actually climb him, wrapping my legs around his waist and holding on tight, the thick length of his cock pressing between my thighs so sweet I buck and moan.

"Can't wait, can you baby? Need me to make that ache all better?"

"Yes," I moan, rubbing up against him again.

He gives me a dangerous smile. "You need to be careful what you wish for."

He turns and strides through the apartment, making straight for his bedroom. My pulse races with anticipation. We both know where this is heading. No more teasing, no fooling around.

I'm getting fucked, and God, I can't wait.

He shoves open the door, and I find myself deposited onto the bed. I reach for him hungrily. My blood is roaring with desire, and all I can think about is getting both of us naked.

But Nero has other plans.

He captures my wrists, pinning my hands above my head. "Don't move."

"W-what?"

He smirks above me, and God, it's sexy.

"You're not touching me, not yet. Not until I've had my fill of this body."

I want to protest, but his lips are on mine again, and he releases my wrists to touch me—everywhere. He cups my breasts, plucking the hardened buds of my nipples even through my dress. I moan out loud, a pulsing ache rising between my thighs, making me writhe.

I need him.

As if he's reading my mind, Nero moves me so I'm straddling his lap. His hands grip my ass, and he grinds up against me, the hard ridge of his cock pressing at my core, rubbing my clit just right.

I whimper in delight. God, he's going make me come, and we're not even naked yet.

Impatient, I reach for him, trying to yank his shirt open and run my hands over his chest. His body is so magnificent, I need to touch. I need to taste him. But Nero makes a sound of amusement, and this time, he grabs my wrists more forcefully.

I stare down at him, breathless.

"We've just started and you're already breaking the rules," he muses, his voice a low, sexy growl. "Do you *want* to be punished?"

Punished. My pulse kicks with excitement at the idea. Just what would that mean...? "Maybe," I answer, teasing. "What are you going to do about it?"

Nero's eyes darken. "Naughty girl."

He lands a quick smack on my ass, making me yelp. "Now hush," he orders me. "This body of yours has been aching for me, and you can bet I'm making up for lost time."

He pulls my dress up, over my head, and I eagerly help him with the task, leaving me in just my white lace bra and panties, kneeling on the bed beside him.

Nero's gaze rakes over me, making me shudder with awareness. He lets out a low grown. "Fuck, baby... Take off your bra. Show me those perfect tits."

I reach for the front clasp of the bra, opening it with a flick of my wrist. My nipples grow harder as the cool air in the room hits them. Nero's tongue darts out and licks his lips.

"You want to touch something so bad?" he asks, eyes flashing with barely controlled lust. "Touch yourself, Princess. Play with your nipples. Show me where you want my mouth."

I do as he orders, running my thumbs across my nipples and sucking in a sharp breath at the feeling.

Nero leans in, following my touch and giving my breasts a slow lick. He sucks on one nipple, then pulls off, his mouth making an obscene wet pop. *Oh God.* He pulls his shirt over his head and starts to open his pants. When he pushes his jeans down, his erection springs free, thick and straining.

Fuck. I run my eyes over him greedily, taking in the well-defined chest and abdomen, all lean muscle and tattoos. His body is a work of art, and as for his cock...

My mouth waters, watching him fist his thick length in his hand. He smiles lazily. "You've missed this beast, haven't you, baby?"

"*Yes,*" I breathe. I can't lie to him. The nights I've spent, reliving my first time with him. Imagining what he would be like now, how he would take me, continue the lessons in pleasure we only just begun. "I need you, God, so bad."

Nero's expression flashes with victory, and then faster than I can process, I'm suddenly on my back beneath him. "That's because this pussy knows it belongs to me," he growls, palming between my legs, making me moan. "Now tell me I can fuck it bare."

My mind is so full of lust, it takes me a second to realize what he means. "Yes, I'm on the pill," I gasp, writhing beneath him. "Nero, please..."

"No going back, baby," Nero rears up above me, wild-eyed and magnificent. He grips my panties and rips them off my body like they were paper. I feel a shock of realization, understanding for the first time how much he's been holding himself back.

And what it means to see him finally unleashed.

"You're going to give me everything," he growls, roughly spreading my thighs. "Daddy's home."

He holds me down and fucks into me, all the way to the hilt.

Fuck!

I scream in pleasure, just about losing my mind at the thick intrusion, thrusting deep. *God, so deep.* Nero lets out a guttural noise, and for a moment, we're suspended there. Not moving.

Joined again.

I flex, my body trying to adjust to the sheer girth of him, and Nero groans again. "Fuck, baby, I can't wait—"

"So don't," I say breathlessly. I clench around him, already needing more friction. Needing more of him. Everything my body has been aching for. Everything I've been missing all these years. "Don't hold back." I tell him, desperate. "Don't be gentle. Just *take me*."

Nero rears up and fucks me into the sheets.

Yes!

I arch up to meet his thrusts, wrapping my legs around his waist. He slams into me again, deeper, *harder*, filling me up, and fuck, I can't take it, it's just too good. My mind shuts down, the world disappears, and all that's left is the hot groan of his panting and the high-pitched sound of my moans, and the slick, damp drive of his body, fucking me with a force that shakes the bed and sends my body jolting with impact.

I hurtle towards a climax before I even realize. I can't hold it back. "Oh my God—"

Nero growls, feeling my body clench around him. "What's wrong, baby? Not used to a man who gets you there, every fucking time?"

He reaches between us, rubbing my clit swiftly, and fuck, my body can't take the added sensation. I climax all over again with a cry.

"Nero!" I clutch the sheets, shocked by my own response. I've never come so fast, so often.

But he doesn't look surprised. He smiles down at me with a dangerous power in his eyes. "That's right," he drawls, lazily stroking where our bodies are joined. He fucks me slowly through the ripples of pleasure. "Say my name. Scream it, baby. Tell the whole city who's making this tight pussy go off."

As I'm gasping for breath, shaken by my orgasms, Nero flips us, settling back against the pillows with me straddling his lap. "Ride me, Princess," he orders me, positioning his dick below my dripping entrance. "Take your pleasure. I want to watch you go to town on my dick."

His filthy words make me flush, but God, I love it all.

Panting, I sink down on his cock, slowly taking him inside me.

God, the new angle is something else. He spears up inside me, deeper than ever, hitting that special spot that makes me see stars.

I toss my head back and moan.

"Fuck yeah," Nero groans. He's heavy-lidded below me, gripping my hips as he thrusts up inside. "Look at you, taking it all. Such a fucking good girl for me."

He lands a loud slap on my bare ass, making me jerk.

"That's right, make those gorgeous tits bounce." Nero spanks me again, urging me on. "Go to town, baby. The beast's all yours."

The truth is, I've never ridden on top before. I'm not even sure where to begin, so I inhale a shuddering breath, rising up a little, and then quickly sinking back down. His groan of appreciation gives me new confidence, so I do it again. Faster. Harder. Until I'm bouncing on his cock, loving the friction and the way Nero is groaning in pleasure beneath me. I rake my nails over his chest, circling my hips to grind just right.

"Fuck, you're a miracle," he gasps, breath ragged. I can feel the muscles of his hard body flex and release as he moves with me. Even in this position, we both know who holds the power here. "So tight, just like I remembered. Only you. My Lily."

I moan, another orgasm building inside me. This one is gathering like a tidal wave, and the power of it almost scares me. I falter, my motions fading. "Nero..." I whimper.

"I've got you, baby." He thrusts up inside me, directing my movements now, and all I can do it go along with it. His hold on my hips is tight that it'll probably leave bruises, but I don't care. "I've always got you. Did any other man ever make you feel like this?"

"No," I cry. "No one. Never!"

"That's right. Because you're *mine*."

He thrusts up again with a roar, sending me hurtling over the edge. I come apart with a scream, my body convulsing with the force of my orgasm, ripping through me in wave after wave of intense pleasure. I lose all sense of everything other than him. All that matters is this, as below me, I feel Nero stiffen, and then climax with his own animal groans of ecstasy, pumping into me, fucking me through every breath.

I collapse onto his chest, my body exhausted. Holy hell. I gasp for air, reeling at the feelings still crashing through my body, aftershocks of pleasure chasing the last ebb of my climax away.

What the hell *was* that?

Calling it sex seems like a disservice. It's never been like this with anyone. Even my first time with Nero couldn't compare to what we just did and up until now, that had been the best I'd ever had.

But he was right. It was nothing compared to the man he is now.

NERO FALLS ASLEEP, spooning there beside me in the bed with my head tucked underneath his chin and his arms draped around me, holding me close for hours in the night.

I don't sleep. I can hear his heart beating, feeling the steady rhythm of his breathing. My own breathing automatically lines up with him, and I can feel my body relax, despite the first strands of doubt beginning to stir in my mind.

What am I doing here?

Sex was crossing the line enough, but laying here in his arms, listening to him breathe, reveling in the luxury of his embrace? I feel warm, *protected*.

But I know, it can't last.

Nothing has changed, even if everything feels different now.

Suddenly restless, I slide out of bed. I grab his robe from the back of the door, and creep out of the room. The apartment is silent, bathed in the light from the kitchen counter, and there's plenty of space in the huge loft, but it's not enough.

I head to the stairs and climb upwards. I know they lead to the rooftop, and right now, I need some air. Somewhere to gather my thoughts—away from Nero's sleeping body.

I push open the door and step outside. Nero owns the whole building, and the rooftop stretches out, with an awning and lounge furniture, offering breathtaking views of the city around us, glittering in the dawn light. There's a chill in the air, but I find it refreshing. Besides, Nero's robe is so long that it brushes the ground, and the sleeves cover my hands.

I take a seat on one of the daybeds, looking out over the city. It's beautiful, white and yellow lights coming from tall buildings set against an inky sky. I've always loved it. It's home.

But being here with Nero?

It feels *too much* like home.

I loved him so much when I was younger. I would have done anything for him. If I'd been given a choice when my dad went into witness protection, I wouldn't have gone. I would have stayed—with him. No matter what.

And of course, it would have been the end of me. Because no matter what Nero and I wanted, it wasn't our choice, our world. Our fathers were the ones calling the shots. Mine, betraying the crooked organization he'd profited from, and Roman Barretti, out for blood, the way he always was.

And here Nero is, following in his footsteps.

I shiver. Would he really go through with it? Make an

example of me and my brother, to send a message. If this vote doesn't go his way, if I can't get McKenna on board...

Would Nero look me in the eyes and pull the trigger? After everything.

After tonight.

I feel a desperate ache in my chest. I know I'm a fool for blurring all the lines, and letting desire send me right back into his arms, but it's like I can't help myself. The heart wants what it wants, and I have to admit to myself that mine has always belonged to Nero.

However stupid that may be.

I don't know how long I sit there, turning it all over in my mind. The sun is rising when I hear a noise behind me and turn to see Nero join me. He's only wearing pajama pants, but he doesn't seem to be cold.

"Hey," he says softly, taking a seat beside me. He wraps his arms around me, holding me in a warm embrace. "I wondered where you went."

"Just wanted to watch the sunrise." I gesture to the horizon, where the sky is painted in shades of blue, purple, pink, and orange.

"I don't think I've ever been up here," Nero looks around.

"It really is beautiful," I say.

"Yes. It is."

When I turn to look at him, Nero is watching me with a new intensity burning in his eyes, just as vivid as the sunrise in the sky.

My heart catches.

It's not just desire between us anymore, it's more than that, I know.

"Nero..." I start to say, but he stops me.

"Shh... Don't say it. Let's have tonight, Lily. Give me tonight."

So I do.

Nero's hand comes up to cup my cheek and he presses his lips to mine. I melt into the kiss, all of the uncertainty of the last few hours finally fleeing my mind as I go with my instinct.

With gentle nudging, Nero lays me back on the daybed. The robe parts as I shift, and his hand slips inside. He traces my bare skin with his fingertips, and I tremble under the light touch, electricity shooting across my body with every caress as he whispers over my breasts, my belly, dipping lightly between my thighs before tracing back up again. I moan in pleasure, but it's a different kind to the raw, animal lust that's fueled us so far. Soft. Luxurious.

He kisses me softly, as I finally explore the planes of his body, stroking his muscular back with my hands, drifting over the curve of his ass, the smooth skin warm under my fingers. He's being so tender with me, I barely breathe, not wanting to break the spell as Nero's tongue delves into my mouth. He finds the belt of the robe and unties it, exposing my body to the early morning sun. It's exhilarating, and I spread myself beneath him like an offering.

Nero bends his head, and licks over my breasts. We're out in the open air, but that doesn't stop a moan from escaping me as he suckles on my nipples, alternating between flicking his tongue over the stuff bud and sucking on it until it's taut and aching.

"God, you're so beautiful," he murmurs, worshipping me with his eyes, his hands, his tongue. "I could look at you forever."

His mouth moves to my other breast, and he takes his time giving it just as much attention. It feels so good, but now my warm desire has changed into a blistering arousal. I writhe beneath him as his efforts with my nipples drive me crazy.

"Nero," I whimper. "Please..."

"Always," he vows. "Your man will always give you what you need."

I part my legs wider and brace myself for his rough intrusion, but instead, Nero keeps kissing me softly, slowly moving down my body, lavishing attention to every inch of me until I'm squirming.

Nero pauses at the end of the daybed, eyes dark as he strokes over me, teasing my clit. He dips a finger in my wetness and brings it to his lips to lick clean. "I already know your cunt is delicious," he says, his voice thick with lust. "I've been going crazy for another taste."

I freeze, my heart pounding. *Is he going to...?*

"Yeah, I am," he replies, reading the question in my eyes. "Your man's going to lick that sweet pussy until you're screaming. Because fuck, baby, I've got to feel you drip that sugar all over my tongue."

I'm still reeling from the sexy promise when Nero settles between my thighs and licks up against me in a hot, mind-blowing swoop.

Oh my god!

"Nero!" I cry out, already lost to the rush of it. His tongue is lapping, probing, swirling over my sensitive bud just right as *oh*, he sinks one thick finger and then another inside me and starts to thrust.

It's a devastating combination, stimulating me inside and out, and soon—*fuck, too soon*—I'm wound tight, the summit in sight. "Don't stop," I chant, reaching down to rake my fingers in his hair, bucking mindlessly at his mouth. "God, please don't stop."

"Fuck, baby, I'm just getting started."

Nero shoves me back, pinning me with his free hand as the other works its wicked magic, flexing his fingers high inside me; his tongue lapping hard at my clit. I sob in pleasure, writhing, out of my mind. He's devouring me, there's no other way to describe it, facedown in my pussy like a starving man making a mess of his last meal. Every lick and rub sends me higher, careening to the edge, and when he closes his lips around the bud of my clit and suckles—

I come apart with a scream.

Fuck. *Fuck.* My orgasm washes over me in waves, as Nero holds me down, one hand on my stomach, grounding me in place as my body shakes and trembles beneath his wicked tongue.

"Mine."

I lift my head, dazzled, to find him watching me there in the dawn light.

"Say it," he demands, the words a low growl on his lips.

My heart stutters.

"Yours," I whisper. And I know in my bones, it's true. I belong to him.

But can I trust him?

21

LILY

AFTER SPENDING SUCH an earth-shaking night in Nero's arms, it seems impossible that I would wake up in exactly the same world the next morning, but that's exactly what happens. He goes to work, I take a shower, and spend the day working on my painting, and counting down the hours until I can have him alone again.

Then Nero calls with news. "I swung us an invite to dinner with McKenna and his wife tonight," he says.

"What?" I blink. "That's amazing, how did that happen?"

"Guess we hit it off, after all," he replies. "Either that, or he's ready to hit me up for a campaign donation."

"The timing couldn't be better," I say, but Nero just grunts.

"Yeah, we'll see about that. I'll pick you up at six, we're dining at their place in Syosset," he says, naming a rich town just outside the city.

"And it's just the four of us?"

"Yup. Real cosy," Nero replies. I hang up and go pick out our wardrobe for the night. As much as I'm relieved Nero's plan to get close to McKenna is paying dividends, I also hate the reminder of the deal hanging over my head.

If Nero gets McKenna to fold and rubber-stamp the development deal, then I'll have fulfilled my part of the bargain. I'll be free.

But what about Nero and me?

I push the question aside, as Nero picks me up, and we head out to the McKennas' that evening.

Nero seems wound even more tightly than usual, his knee bobbing behind the steering wheel on the drive over. He probably knows this may be our last shot to make this happen before the vote.

My last shot to win my brother's safety.

I swallow and turn my attention to the surroundings as we pull up the driveway. I whistle. "Wow, what happened to McKenna's story of being just another humble guy made good?"

The house is stately as hell, with three stories, square windows and round columns holding up the porch roof. The white color sticks out from all the green surrounding it: perfectly manicured bushes, rolling lawn, and trees at the far rear of the property. "This is not humble, by any means."

"Good." Nero replies, getting out of the car. He adjusts his jacket, and takes it all in. "Guys with a taste for the finer things need a way to pay for it, after all."

I try to ignore the fact I'm here, helping with something that is definitely immoral, let alone illegal.

We're just approaching the front steps, when my phone buzzes in my bag. I pull it out to silence it, when I realize that it's the wrong one. I grabbed my burner phone on the way out the door, not the one Nero gave me.

Teddy's calling. And I have a dozen missed calls and texts from him in the last ten minutes. Fuck.

Nero hasn't noticed yet, so I angle it in my hand. "It's Marissa," I lie, "Let me just talk to her for a quick sec. She might have useful info about the McKennas," I add.

Nero nods. "Sure."

I turn away, and drop my voice as I answer, my heart racing. "Hello?"

"Hey," Teddy says.

"What's up?" I ask, as Nero checks his own device.

"Well.... Don't panic—" Teddy starts, and I do, immediately.

"Oh God, what is it?" I demand. "Are you okay?"

"I'm fine. I promise." Teddy swears. "It's just that... I got mugged."

"What?"

Nero looks up at my exclamation. I swallow back my panic.

"It's no big deal," Teddy continues. "Just some local thugs that jumped me on my way home last night."

"Why didn't you call me sooner?"

"There's nothing you could do. Like I said, it was just some local jerks. Didn't even take the whole wallet, just pocketed my cash and left."

"Were you hurt?" I whisper, dropping my voice even more.

"Just took a punch to the gut when I tried to refuse to hand over the money, but I'll be okay. Listen, I gotta go, but I knew that you'd want to know what happened. Don't worry about me, okay?"

He hangs up, and I try to collect myself. Mugged? The idea of Teddy in any danger made me feel sick.

"Everything OK?" Nero rejoins me.

I plaster on a smile. "Yup! Marissa's great."

"And Teddy?" he asks, giving me a look. "How's he doing?"

Busted.

"Pretty shaken up, to tell the truth," I keep my head held

high, even if I'm freaking out inside. "He got mugged last night. Roughed up by a group of guys. You wouldn't know anything about that, would you?"

Nero's jaw clenches. "I don't even know where Teddy is," he points out, his voice cold. "But even if I did, we have a deal. He's under my protection, as long as you play your part. Are you saying I'm not a man of my word?"

I exhale. "No. I'm sorry, I just... Freaked out, hearing he was hurt." I shake my head, trying to put it all aside—for the next few hours, at least. "Let's go in," I nod to the front door. "They're probably wondering what's taking us so long."

Nero gives a curt nod, and I follow him to the door. He knocks, and a moment later, Fiona opens it, smiling widely.

"Welcome! I'm so happy you could make it, last minute like this."

"Of course," Nero greets her with a kiss on the cheek. "We wouldn't miss it for the world."

I'm impressed. There's no sign of the growling, resentful guy I took to that first gala. Nero's turned on the charm in an instant and is already complimenting Fiona on the décor as she shows us to a lavish lounge area. "The kids are at a sleepover, and Ian should be right down from a call—ah, here he is!"

Ian strides into the room, relaxed and handsome in a button-down and chinos. "Nero," he says, greeting him with a slap on the back. "Is that your Aston Martin out front? Now that's a nice ride."

"Oh, don't get him talking cars," Fiona interrupts. "He'll be at it all night."

"After dinner," Ian says with a wink. "I'll give you a tour of my garage. I have a collection."

"Deal," Nero replies.

My nerves ease a little. It's all going great so far: Relaxed and friendly.

"Can I offer you a cocktail?" Fiona asks.

"Fifi here makes a great whiskey sour," Ian adds.

"That sounds wonderful," I say.

I take a moment to look around as we all take seats on the couches. The interior of the house is warm and inviting. Natural wood trim and neutral wall colors make the place feel comfortable, but there are things to remind you that this is a place belonging to the wealthy.

The rug beneath our feet is Persian with an ornate pattern made of gold thread. It probably cost more than my last car. There's an original Marie Faulkner painting on the wall next to the river rock fireplace, and the chandelier above us is a true work of art.

All these little things paint quite a picture.

The conversation is light, and I find myself admiring again how far Nero had come in the last few weeks, shooting the shit with Ian about sports and some local city history.

I'm proud of him, but I also like knowing that he's not really a socialite. When I was a teenager, that was the reason I was drawn to him in the first place. All the boys I spent time with were rich boarding school brats. Being born with a silver spoon in your mouth can bring a sense of entitlement that is unappealing to say the least.

Hell, I was even like that. But Nero brought me down to Earth. He showed me that there was more to life than fancy clothes and lunches with the girls. He was *real*.

He still is. Underneath this oozing charm, he's still the same guy, which is why I can't stay away.

"I love your earrings," I tell Fiona. She has a cluster of diamonds surrounding a large ruby in each earlobe. They complement her red dress perfectly. I have to admit, I like her style. "Are they Cartier?"

Fiona smiles, her fingers going to her ear. "Sterling Cross, actually. Ian got them for me on our tenth wedding anniversary."

She beams at her husband, and I can see the love shining in her eyes. This is my first time interacting with the couple privately like this, and I can see just how much she loves him.

I think of my suspicions about Brittany and Ian and try not to wince.

Beatrice comes in to announce that dinner is ready, and we all move into the dining room. Nero pulls my chair out, just as McKenna does the same for his wife. There are salads on the table in front of us and Beatrice comes around with a bottle of insanely expensive wine to pour into our glasses.

I take a sip of it, prepared to complement it as well, but Nero speaks first.

"So, Ian, I know that the zoning board is meeting in a few days to make a decision on my property. Can I count on your vote?"

His request is so abrupt that I nearly choke on my wine. I send him a silent look. What the hell is he playing at? I thought he understood that he can't be that direct with this man.

The atmosphere in the dining shifts on a dime, becoming thick with tension. Fiona's eyes are darting back and forth between the two men while McKenna looks almost offended. "Well, really..." he splutters. "I certainly wasn't expecting this. It's quite inappropriate."

Nero shrugs. "I'm sick of beating around the bush. I figure, let's cut the bullshit, talk straight, and then enjoy a good meal." He sits back, looking supremely confident. Like this is his house.

Like McKenna is already in his pocket.

But the politician has other ideas. "If you must force the issue, then... No. I won't be supporting you with my vote. Nothing personal against you," he adds, "But I need to think of appearances. It would be political suicide to go on the record supporting you. Hell, they'd crucify me for the rest of my political career. Say I was in bed with a *Barretti*."

His voice drips with disdain, and I flinch, expecting Nero to lose his shit.

But Nero just gives a relaxed shrug.

"Appearances, huh?" he says, reaching into the inner pocket of his suit. "Funny you should be so worried about associating with me. When it's your other *associations* that might do more to hurt your political ambitions."

Nero pulls out a sheaf of photographs and tosses them one-by-one on the polished dining room table for us all to see.

I gasp. They're surveillance photos, showing Ian—and Brittany. In some luxury hotel, together. Shot through an open strip in the drapes, in the throes of passion. Naked on the bed, Brittany riding him, her bare breasts bouncing. Ian fucking her from behind over the bed. On his knees, eating her out.

Fiona makes a noise of distress, clapping a hand over her mouth. I can see her heart breaking, and I want to tell Nero not to do this, but my voice is caught in my throat. It's like watching a train wreck. I can't look away.

"Tell me, Ian," Nero continues, voice so friendly, it sends a chill down my spine. "How do you think a dirty affair will play with the voters? Think they'll still show out for you on election day when they learn you've been fucking your side piece all over the city? Not that I blame you," he adds. "She's a real fine piece of ass, isn't she? But I don't need to tell you that, you're clearly an ass man. Wait, let me find it..."

He flips through the photos until he pulls one showing Ian on all fours on the bed.

And Brittany, behind him, fucking his ass with a strap-on.

Fiona lets out a devastated sob, standing so abruptly that her chair topples over. Her eyes are wild that they dart around to each of us, her chest heavy. It's horrifying to watch a woman that's always so put together coming completely undone.

"Fiona—"

The sound of McKenna saying her name seems to trigger something inside of her and she spins on her heel before fleeing the room.

"Fiona!" This time McKenna shouts her name as bolts after her. We hear the sound of frantic footsteps on the stairs, followed by the slamming of a door—and then yelling, and pleading voices.

I sit there, stunned, at the empty table. "I can't believe you just did that," I tell Nero, reeling.

"It worked, didn't it?"

He takes another gulp of wine, like it's no big deal. I can hear Fiona crying upstairs and McKenna knocking on the door, begging to be let in.

"What is wrong with you?" I exclaim, furious. I push back my chair and get to my feet. "Why did you have to do that in front of Fiona? She didn't deserve that. If the guy's a cheating bastard, then why didn't you threaten him in private?"

Nero narrow his eyes. "Because he'll take it seriously now. And because she'll be the one telling him to vote my way, so these photos don't get out and humiliate her even more."

I can't believe this. "You disgust me," I tell him, heading for the door. I'm guessing we won't be invited to stay for dessert.

Nero catches up to me in the foyer. "What did you expect?" he demands, grabbing my arm and turning me to face him. "That I'd ask nicely? Say 'please,' when the guy looks down his nose at me like that? Fuck no," he vows. "I'm a lion, not a goddamn lamb."

I try to pull free. "That was cruel," I tell him.

"And that's who I am," Nero growls, his expression dark. He backs me up against the wall, until I'm crushed against him, his voice low in my ear. "I'm cruel, and ruthless, and I'll do whatever it takes to get what I want. You just can't admit you like me this way."

I shake my head, even as my pulse kicks with excitement. "I don't."

"Oh yeah?" Nero trails a hand over my breast, squeezing roughly. I shudder. "You're lying to yourself," he says with a cruel smirk. "It makes you hot, seeing this side of me. The king who takes what he wants."

"You're wrong." My voice wavers with desire. *Fuck*. He's right. I can't even deny it like I mean it. Watching him dominate every room he walks into.

Watching him dominate *me*.

Nero's smile grows. "Is that so? Because I think if I shove that dress up around your waist, you'll be wet and ready for me. If I tell you to get on your knees right now, you'll do it, just hit the floor and open that sweet mouth and beg to suck my cock."

I gasp, as Nero yanks me into a nearby coat closet and slams the door. Suddenly, I'm pressed up against him in the dark, his mouth on mine.

Yes.

I sink into the kiss, already hot and reeling.

Then he pulls back, spins me around, and shoves me face-first against the wall. "Hands up, baby," he growls in my ear from behind me, his weight pinning me in place. "Let's see about that bet of mine..."

I do as he says, laying my palms flat on the wall above my head as Nero pulls up my dress, bunching it around my waist. He delves into my silk panties with one hand as the other firmly massages my breasts. It feels incredible.

I sink back into his arms, moaning, as he gives a low chuckle of victory, fingers dipping into my slick folds. "Look at you, you're drenched."

He rubs my clit with the heel of his hand, making me whimper. Then he pulls out his hand and thrusts his fingers in my mouth. "Taste it," he orders me, his voice thrillingly firm. "Taste how much you want me."

I let out a moan around his fingers, licking them like he says, and tasting myself. *Fuck, he's too hot.* Touching me in a stranger's house, ordering me around. I can't even see his face; I'm pinned against the wall in the dark with his breath hot in my ear and the thick length of his erection digging into my hip.

"See, I know you, Princess," Nero tells me, as I hear the sound of his belt buckle, and then a zip. "You can walk around playing the perfect socialite, making small talk and smiling like butter wouldn't melt in that hot little mouth of yours, but I know you, all your deep, dark secrets. I know what this cunt really needs."

He grips my hips back, clamps a hand over my mouth, and then slams inside me.

Holy hell!

I scream against his hand, reeling from the delicious force of his thrust. His thick cock drives into me, grinding so deep, it's like I'm being impaled.

"You want to be owned." Nero pulls back, then thrusts again, even deeper. I whimper, arching back to meet him, and he lets out a curse. "Fuck, you want to beg for it. You want it hard and dirty, until you can't even remember your own name."

He slams into me, finding a hard, relentless rhythm that hits me just right. With one hand gripping my breast and the other still muffling my whimpers of pleasure, there's no escaping the hot, dirty grind; his animal grunts filling the dark closet.

All I can do is take it.

And I do, over and over, reveling in the sheer perfection of his dominant thrusts, my body spiraling higher with every earth-shaking thrust, until I break apart with a frenzied cry.

"That's right, baby," Nero growls, pistoning faster as I spasm with my climax in his arms. "Love to feel you clenching on my cock. Milk me out, take it all." He thrusts again, again, and then comes with a roar, spurting deep inside me as we both ride out the waves of pleasure.

Oh. My. God.

He releases me, and I stumble forwards, needing the wall to hold me up, because holy shit, I don't think I'll be walking for a week.

It was just that good.

I hear a zip and turn to find Nero buckling his belt back up. "We should go," he says, looking satisfied, his labored breath the only hint of what we just did. "Probably outstayed our welcome already."

"Uh uh," I manage to murmur. Nero pauses and reaches over to straighten up my dress. He brushes my hair from my eyes, then drops a swift kiss on my forehead.

"C'mon."

He opens the closet door and doesn't even pause to check if anyone's there before striding out. I have no choice but to duck after him. I hightail it to the front door—but not before seeing the housekeeper in the hallway, watching us disapprovingly. With my hair mussed and my dress askew, I could be wearing a billboard saying, 'I just fucked in a closet.'

I follow Nero to the car and tumble in, feeling the desire fade under a wash of shame and embarrassment. What just happened? Upstairs, Fiona McKenna is probably weeping, her entire life crumbling before her eyes.

We did that.

I did that.

Nero starts the engine. "All in all, I'd say that went pretty well, don't you?" he shoots me a triumphant grin as we drive away.

I feel a chill.

He's proud of what just went down, I realize in horror. He doesn't care about the collateral damage, or who he hurts along the way. He'll do anything to get what he wants—just like he's been warning me.

Nero Barretti has been telling me exactly who he is from the start, I've just been trying to ignore the truth that's right in front of me.

"I'm cruel, and ruthless, and I'll do whatever it takes to get what I want."

His words echo, loud in my mind. He means them, every last one.

So what happens if I get in the way of that? I wonder, when it's *me* standing between him and the next part of his Barretti empire expansion.

Will me and my brother wind up as collateral damage, just like Ian and Fiona?

Can I even trust him to honor our arrangement, when he's so proud of the fact he's a man without honor?

What was I thinking, making a deal with the devil?

The devil always wins.

I look at him sitting beside me, and for the first time, he looks like a stranger to me.

Dread sinks through me. I've always believed Nero is a man of his word, but how true is it?

I can't believe I've come this far, managed to dance around my certain death and play Nero at his own game, only to let my heart risk everything by falling back in love with him. The kind of foolish love that made me forget how much is at stake.

That made me ignore what kind of man Nero really is.

The King of the Barretti empire.

It will always come first—not me. It will always enjoy his utter loyalty—not me.

As much as it pains me to realize it, I finally understand the truth. He can't be trusted, no matter how much I want it to be different this time.

I'm on my own.

And I know exactly what I have to do.

22

LILY

"LEFT TO THE MAIN EXHIBIT, and remember, to keep to the marked lines away from the paintings."

I take a deep breath and try to settle the nerves fluttering in my stomach as I stroll slowly through the main floor at the Met. It's busy today, and I blend in among the crowd as I look at their exhibits, taking in the beautiful art. It makes sense that I would visit this place. I'm an artist, after all, which is why I breezily told Nero over breakfast I was going to pay a visit.

"There's a new Rothko exhibit," I joked, "But I'm sure it won't hold a candle to yours."

He barely looked up from his phone. "Sure. Fine."

He's been busy since the McKenna dinner, lining up the final pieces of his deal. I'm glad, because it hasn't given him a chance to notice my anxiety, as I made my way to the museum, and walked in past security, my heart in my throat.

I'm here to meet the FBI.

This time, I was the one who reached out—calling the agent number I memorized from a payphone across from my yoga studio. I gave them a day and time, but even so, I haven't been certain that I'll actually show up.

Because once I make this deal... There's no going back.

I linger in front of a series of paintings from the early nineteenth century, trying to delay my choice. They're landscapes, and utterly beautiful. I can't help wondering if I would have ever been featured in a museum if my art career had been allowed to flourish. Would I have seen one hung in a palace like this? Become a well-known name in the art world?

It's impossible to know what would have happened if things were different, and I know that I've got to stop dwelling on what-ifs. Life is happening right now, and it's up to me to make the right call.

Right now, I'm looking at two equally bad options, and I have to choose a path. Put my trust in Nero—or the Feds. I wonder for a second if this is what my dad felt when he became an informant. He never talked much about what led him to the decision, but I assume he thought it was the right choice.

He did it to protect us. Now, I need to think of Teddy.

Taking a deep breath, I turn away from the gallery hall, and head down a series of hallways. Half-hidden away from the main tourist sites, there's a research library with some conference rooms. I bet on it being quieter, and I'm right. There's only a couple of students deep in work, and I make my way to the very back room.

Agent Greggs is waiting for me, with the woman who approached me in the boutique dressing room.

Agent DiMedio.

"Lily," Greggs smiles, greeting me. in fact, they're both smiling. After all, I'm the one who's coming to them this time. They think they're already won. "Sit down. I grabbed some snacks from the cafeteria, if you're hungry." He gestures to the motley collection of vending machine snacks.

I shake my head.

"So, how's it going?" DiMedia asks.

"Let's not do this," I reply. "All the small talk. I told you on the phone, I want to hear how this is going to go. What it is you want, and what you can offer me. No more games."

The two of them exchange a look.

Agent Greggs pulls out a file. "Very well. In exchange for information that leads to the conviction of Nero Barretti, we're willing to strike a deal. Immunity for anything you may know, or have been party to, and witness protection for you—and your brother."

"We'll set him up in college somewhere," DiMedio adds, "and find you a job and an apartment nearby. You'll have a team assigned to you, protection for the first couple of years, and then ad hoc. If we get word that the Barrettis know about your new identities, we'll move you again, whatever it takes."

My heart sinks, hearing it laid out for me like this. I was hoping for something better, but it's the same deal my father took—and look how it turned out for him.

"Look, I know you've been through this already," Agent Greggs says, leaning forward. "But this will be different.

I've pulled some strings. No more shitty small towns, you can pick where you want to go. Austin, maybe. Seattle. Portland. We'll find you work in an art gallery or a museum, Teddy will be in a great school. And we can give you a small settlement, to get you started. Not a fortune, but enough to give you options. But most importantly, you'll be safe. Both of you will."

He's saying all the right things. The guy has clearly done his homework about me. But I can't shake this uneasy feeling that wherever we went, Nero would find us. Somehow.

He found me in Vegas. Yeah, it was an accident, but it still happened. And I can't trust that the FBI will keep me safe. They are not all incorruptible, and if I've learned anything over the last few weeks, it's that Nero will find a way to find a weak spot and exploit it.

Maybe he already has. Maybe one of the agents looking back at me has already cut a deal, ready to tell him everything the minute I make my move.

Paranoia? Maybe. But that's the life I'm looking at, another sixty years of checking the shadows and watching the door.

"I'll have to think about it," I tell them. "It's a big risk."

Agent Greggs rises and shows me to the door.

"Listen, Lily. I know that things weren't great for you after your dad turned on Barretti, but I don't want you to focus on that. Think about what the right thing to do is. Think about whether or not you feel safe around him. Trusting us is a risk—but we both know, trusting Nero is a bigger one."

I gulp. "I'll let you know soon," I promise.

"Don't wait too long," Greggs warns me. "We're moving on Nero soon, with or without your testimony. And if you're still at his side when we do... I won't be able to get you out."

I hurry away from the room, moving blindly back to the main halls. I hoped this meeting would give me some clarity, but it's more confusing than ever. I'm trapped between a rock and a hard place.

What do you do when there's no good way out?

I sigh. Maybe the answer is neither of them. Hell, maybe the best way out is just to disappear on my own, and pray to God that neither of them find me. I'd be running, but Teddy could stay where he is, and if Nero's deal comes through, he won't have the time or patience to come after me.

It's a pipe dream, I know, and even with my mind set on leaving, my heart still gives a traitorous ache at the idea of walking away from Nero.

But I'll do what I have to in order to survive.

This time, I'll need a plan. I can't just bolt and expect it to work out for me. I'll need ID, money, a way to get out. My mind is already racing as

"I'll have to think about it," I say, but I've already made my decision.

I think Greggs can tell that it's a no, but he nods anyway.

"Fine. I'll be in touch in a few days."

Getting out of his chair, he comes around the table. I stand and he holds his hand out to me. I take it, expecting a quick shake, but he sandwiches my hand between two of his and meets my eyes.

Great. He's still trying to connect with me.

This guy doesn't give up easily.

"Listen, Lily. I know that things weren't great for you after your dad turned on Barretti, but I don't want you to focus on that. Think about what the right thing to do is. Think about whether or not you feel safe around him. Can you trust him?"

He keeps holding onto my hand, as if he expects an actual answer, but I don't give him one. I simply yank my hand away as I open the door and take a step backward.

"You've given me plenty to think about already. Thanks."

I head for the exit, and my phone buzzes in my pocket.

It's Nero.

I want you on your knees for me.

My pulse kicks, despite everything.

I'm playing it smart, I tell myself, to excuse the desire in my bloodstream. I need time to get this plan of mine together, so I need to act like nothing's changed. Like I trust him. If I don't respond to him sexually now, he'll ask questions.

Questions I don't have answers to.

At least, that's how I justify it, as I meet his driver and head over to the club.

I'll allow myself to enjoy the pleasure that only Nero can

give me. To surrender to him as many times as I can until morning. It'll give me the memories I need to carry on.

Then, once his vote goes through, I'll be gone, and he can go back to hating me.

When we arrive at the club, I head through the dark hallway towards his office.

I know something is wrong the moment I open the door.

Nero is there, but he's not alone. Chase is standing right behind him, and he's got a satisfied smirk on his stupid face.

I bite back a chill of fear.

"Hey," I greet him with a big smile. "You called. Well, texted. So here I am." I give him a flirty look, praying that his sullen mood is Mob-related business.

"You deceitful *bitch*." Nero's voice is shaking with fury.

I reel back in shock. "What's going on?" I ask, the fear taking root in my whole body. I look to the door, but there's already one of his guys standing there, blocking the exit.

I'm trapped.

"You really need to ask?" Nero's eyes flash angrily. He grabs a page from his desk and tosses it at me.

It flutters to the floor, and I see, it's not a document, but a surveillance photo.

His desk is covered in them.

Oh God.

Taken just a half hour ago, they show me going into the research library—and meeting the FBI. With the door open, Greggs is clearly visible, as well as the agent beside him. Then, there are more photos of me leaving. Greggs is standing right by the door. He's holding onto my hand, deep in conversation as we say goodbye. It looks so damning, as if we're shaking on a deal.

Fuck.

"Listen," I blurt, desperate. "This isn't what it looks—"

"We know who that fucker is," Chase cuts me off. "Did you think we wouldn't recognize the man that put Roman behind bars? Your daddy's little FBI pal?"

"They called *me*," I protest, voice trembling. "They've been trying to make me cut a deal, but I haven't. I wouldn't." I look plaintively at Nero, but there's no emotion in his eyes. He's staring at me like I'm a stranger, completely shut down.

"You can't lie to us. The pictures tell the whole story," Chase sneers. "I told you I'd be watching you, and you went and did this anyway. I had no idea you were this stupid."

"Nero, please!" I beg. "You have to believe me. I helped you with McKenna! I did everything you asked of me!"

But he turns away. "Get her out of here," he growls.

"No!" I cry. "Nero, I swear, I didn't do it!"

I'm still begging when they drag me out, back down the hall to a bare concrete room.

The one they put me that first day, when it all began. But back then, I had a chance. I had something Nero wanted even more than revenge.

Now, I have nothing.

Chase hurls me roughly inside. "Enjoy the view, Princess," he says, grinning. "It's the last one you're going to get."

The door slams shut behind him. There's no escape. No way out.

No way to stop Nero from killing me, the way he's wanted since the moment he laid eyes on me.

I fall to the cold floor, and sob.

23

NERO

"THAT BITCH DIDN'T SEE it coming. Did you hear how she begged?"

Chase is crowing, talking about his big win busting Lily, but I barely hear a word. All I can do is stare at those photos. Her lies right there in front of me in black and white.

I trusted her. I loved her.

And yet again, I was so distracted buried deep in her wet cunt that I didn't see her betrayal coming.

History fucking repeating, all over again.

How could I have been so blind?

"Fuck, we don't know what she's already told them," Chase says, pacing back and forth. "What has she seen?"

I shake my head. "Nothing." I try to keep a grip, even as loathing runs hot in my veins. Demanding answers.

Demanding *violence*.

"You sure about that?" Chase pushes back. "She must have something to offer them. She's been in your apartment, who knows if she's been listening in, copying documents, fuck, going through your shit at night?"

"I don't keep anything there," I growl, so close to losing it, I have my fists clenched.

"Still, we need to take care of this, now. You've got to—"

"*Silence!*" I roar, sweeping the desk clean. A computer and files clatter to the floor, glasses smash, but it's not enough.

I want to tear the whole fucking world down.

Chase takes a step back.

"I'm on your side, man. But she's got to go," he says stubbornly. "Permanently. You need to end her. Make an example. Otherwise..."

He doesn't need to say it. Otherwise, I'll have no damn authority left in this place. I'll be seen as a soft touch. The cunt-struck fool who brought the organization down for a good fuck.

My empire will crumble to the ground.

I have no choice.

"I'll deal with it," I swear, heading for the door.

"Good." Chase nods. "Because I'm guessing Roman has already heard the news. That means every Barretti man in the city will be coming for her."

My father.

The thought alone is enough to send me striding straight past Lily's jail cell. She can wait right there. But my father? If what Chase says is true, I need to deal with him.

Now.

I COLLECT MY CAR, and hit the highway, taking the familiar route up to the low-security prison he's been living in for the last ten years.

The great Roman Barretti. He's been a shadow looming over my life for as long as I can remember. When I was a kid, he was training me to be his heir, always giving me advice and instruction. Reminding me to be ruthless above all things. Even when he got sent down, and I took over, his presence still made himself known. Those first years, he continued running everything from his cell; I was pretty much just his mouthpiece. But as time passed, I've taken the reins.

His ways are the old ways, and I'm looking to the future now. That's what this real estate deal is all about. Not that he knows my plans. He wouldn't understand the direction I'm trying to steer us in, no matter how good the reward. Like Chase, he's old-school. He only understands territory and product, blood and loyalty. So I've kept things to myself.

And I sure as hell never told him about Lily, either.

I arrive, and head in through security, going through the regular routine before I'm shown to a private meeting room. Perks? Yeah, we have this place locked down. My father's in a single, cushy cell, with a flat-screen TV and a guard on our payroll bringing him takeout whenever he wants.

Roman arrives with his usual bodyguards in tow. He's made enough enemies that we keep several guys locked up here with him, round-the-clock protection—for a hefty price.

"Son."

He shuffles into the room. His health took a hit a few years back, but he's still looking sharp: Clean and shaven, with his salt-and-pepper hair slicked back. He takes a seat at the table, and nods to the guard at the door. "Jerry," he says, friendly. "How's the new baby?"

"Keeping the wife up," Jerry replies.

"They always do. Why don't you go grab my son and I a couple of cold sodas," he says, like he's in a fancy restaurant. "We'll be just fine on our own."

Jerry looks around the hallway, then nods.

"Take your time," Roman adds, as he strolls away. His own guards take up position outside the door, and close it.

We're alone.

"So, it's been a while, son," he says, assessing me. His voice is still friendly, but his eyes are cold. "Anything you want to tell me?"

I don't have to tell him a damn thing. He has spies among my men, and they've already filled him in.

But he wants to hear it from me.

"I found Lily Fordham a few weeks ago," I reply, calmer than I feel. Hell, just speaking her name makes me want to burn something to the ground. "Her father's dead. Cancer. We checked it out. It's legit."

Roman exhales, his lips curling in a smile. "Good. That fucker can rot in hell."

He pulls a packet of cigarettes from his jumpsuits, and lights one, taking a long drag. "So, why is the girl still alive? Wait, don't tell me. I hear you two have been getting nice and close."

I don't react. "She's been useful."

"I'm sure she has." Roman's mouth thins. "And now she's being useful to the Feds, just like her whore of a father. You really fucked this one up. Christ, son, what the fuck were you thinking?"

"I know what I'm doing." I refuse to rise to his bait, even though a part of me recoils at his anger. The little kid, still striving for his approval. "I've got it covered."

"Do you?" Roman stands, slamming his hands on the table. "Is this what you call leadership?" he demands, roaring in fury. "Getting your dick wet while shit gets out of hand? I made this organization." He growls. "I built this fucking empire with my own two hands, and I won't stand by and watch you piss it all away!"

I stand. "I'm taking care of it. The Feds have nothing."

"You better hope that's true!" he yells. "Because no son of

mine is going to destroy everything I've worked for. Get your fucking house in order, or I'll do it for you!"

I walk out, with his threat ringing in my ears. He means it, too, and God knows he still has the pull to make it happen. Guys who came up under him, who are loyal to him, no matter what. Any one of them could come for Lily.

Unless I do it first.

Fuck, that girl...

I drive back to the city, my knuckles white on the steering wheel as betrayal forms into a lead weight in my stomach.

She did this. She ruined everything. If she could have just held to our deal, I could have protected her. Been free to love her, the way I've been wanting to half my damn life.

But instead, she stabbed me in the back, like what we've shared meant nothing to her.

And maybe it didn't. Maybe I was the fucking fool, all along.

I think of her up on the rooftop, watching the sun rise. Gold in her hair, cheeks flushed from my cock. Too damn perfect, I couldn't help but fall to my knees and worship her. She was probably laughing at me the whole time.

Counting the minutes until she could deliver me up to the FBI. Send me to prison for the rest of my life.

My father's right. So is Chase. The smartest thing I could do right now is put a bullet right between those pretty blue eyes and end this mockery for good.

But can I do it? Can I really snuff out the light in her soul and leave her body rotting at the bottom of the river?

No matter how much I hate her, how deep her cruel betrayal runs, she's still the only woman I've ever loved.

My Lily.

The lead weight hardens, bringing me a new resolve. I

know what I've been raised to do. Be ruthless. Be smarter than everyone else.

Be willing to do the unthinkable to keep the Barretti empire safe and strong.

There's only one way out of this. My decision is made—and I'm going to see it through.

24

LILY

I LOSE TRACK OF TIME.

I could have been in here. ten hours, or ten days, I don't know. My mind is clouded with fear, I can't think straight. Every time I hear footsteps in the hallway, I shake, wondering if my time is up.

Is this it? Is it all over?

I think of Teddy, and I want to weep. Will he have to mourn me, too? Or, worse, will Nero find him and finish the job?

Wipe the treacherous Fordham family off the map for good.

More footsteps come, and I brace myself. This time, the door opens.

It's Nero. With a gun in his hand.

Oh God.

I'm on the ground, but I don't think my legs could hold me up even if I tried, so I pull myself into a kneeling position.

"Don't waste your time begging, Princess."

Nero's voice is harsh, and cold with betrayal.

I swallow. I can't bear to look at him and see the

wounded cruelty in his eyes. "I never told them anything," I plead again. "We just met, that's all. I wasn't going to betray you."

"But you already did. You lied. You sneaked around. You put my whole empire at risk."

I glance up at that. Nero stands there, looking utterly detached, and I realize with horror that whatever I say now will make no difference.

His mind is made up.

I sag, broken. "Do it," I say, surprised to find tears falling. Not just for my short life, but for Nero, too. Even now, in the midst of my fear, I don't want to make a killer out of him.

I don't want my blood staining his soul.

I take a final look at him, towering there above me. A face I've loved half my life now is harsh and resigned. Eyes burning into me, as dark as night. "You've given me no choice," he swears.

I take deep breath, ready for the end. "Do what you have to do."

I wait for the bullet. The end. But instead, I hear the clatter of metal on the concrete in front of me. Nero has tossed something down into the dirt.

"Pick it up," he orders me.

I scrabble in the dust, wondering what new torture he's devised for me. If this is just delaying the inevitable, or some other twisted game to make me beg.

My fingers brush metal, and I close my hand around it. Small, circular...

It's a ring.

And not just any ring, but a slim gold band.

A wedding ring.

I look up. "What...?" I ask, my terror giving way to confusion. "What is this?"

"Your future." Nero's expression doesn't flinch, as cold as steel. The man who wants me dead.

"Congratulations, Princess," he announces with a sneer. "We're getting married."

I stare at him in disbelief. Take in the cruel triumph in his eyes. And then I realize:

There are some fates worse than death.

TO BE CONTINUED

Lily and Nero's unforgettable love story continues in the next book in the series, Ruthless Games - available to order now!

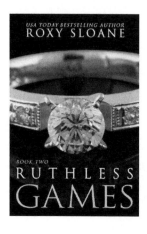

RUTHLESS: BOOK TWO
RUTHLESS GAMES

He was the boy I loved. Now, he's the man who wants me dead.

I struck an impossible bargain to protect the ones I love. I thought I could win his mercy.

But Mafia boss Nero Barretti doesn't know the meaning of the word.

Now, the stakes of this twisted game are higher than ever.

And the passion runs even hotter.

Because it's not just my life on the line anymore.

It's my heart.

CHAPTER ONE: NERO

I'VE HAD this ring waiting for ten goddamn years.

A simple gold band. My mother's ring. I kept it in a box at the back of a dresser drawer, waiting patiently for the day I'd earned the right to slide it on Lily's finger.

Where it belonged.

Back then, it was a sign of my love for her. Our trust. A promise of the brighter tomorrow we could share together.

Now, that future is nothing but darkness. But I'll take it from her, all the same.

I'll take everything she has. And more.

This ring will be a testament to her betrayal. Binding her to me, like her web of lies.

I thought I'd love her forever. Now I'll hate her until the day I die.

My prisoner.

My *wife*.

She has no idea, this is just the beginning.

Roxy Sloane is a USA Today bestselling author, with over 2 million books sold world-wide. Roxy loves indulging her naughty side by writing sinful erotica that pushes the limits. She lives in Los Angeles, and enjoys shocking whoever looks at her laptop screen when she writes in local coffee shops.

www.roxysloane.com
roxy@roxysloane.com

Printed in Great Britain
by Amazon